The Handmaiden's Diary

Bob Williston

The Handmaiden's Diary
Copyright © 2023 by Bob Williston

All rights reserved. No part of this publication may be reproduced, distributed, or transmitted in any form or by any means, including photocopying, recording, or other electronic or mechanical methods, without the prior written permission of the publisher or author, except in the case of brief quotations embodied in critical reviews and certain other noncommercial uses permitted by copyright law.

Although every precaution has been taken to verify the accuracy of the information contained herein, the author and publisher assume no responsibility for any errors or omissions. No liability is assumed for damages that may result from the use of information contained within.

Library of Congress Control Number: 2023920247
ISBN-13: Paperback: 978-1-64749-950-1
Hardcover 978-1-64749-951-8
ePub: 978-1-64749-952-5

Printed in the United States of America

GoToPublish LLC
1-888-337-1724
www.gotopublish.com
info@gotopublish.com

CONTENTS

Dedication v
Thanks vii
Preface ix
Chapter 1 1
Chapter 2 11
Chapter 3 17
Chapter 4 25
Chapter 5 31
Chapter 6 37
Chapter 7 43
Chapter 8 49
Chapter 9 55
Chapter 10 59
Chapter 11 65
Chapter 11 71
Chapter 12 79
Chapter 13 89
Chapter 14 93
Chapter 15 99
Chapter 16 107
Chapter 17 113
Chapter 18 119
Chapter 19 127
Chapter 20 133
Chapter 21 141

Chapter 22 147
Chapter 23 153
Epilogue 157

DEDICATION

The Handmaiden's Diary is dedicated to Angie and her fellow abused handmaidens.

THANKS

Special thanks to Cherie and Chester who read, proofread, and edited me through this project. Their contributions and encouragement were much appreciated. This is not to forget the many others who followed my progress with interest and encouragement.

PREFACE

In Southern California there is a community of an obscure Christian sect commonly called the *Way*. Among those who know members personally, they have a reputation for strict morality and modest living. Way members are not distinguishable from the rest of society by any peculiarity of habit or dress, but two points of doctrine separate them from mainstream Christian churches. One is their weekly worship services, which they hold on Thursday evenings in the homes of their local bishops. The other is their ritual of foot washing, which is performed during their Thursday evening worship service.

The Way was organized somewhere in the Midwest about the year 1900 by a man named John Campbell. Campbell had become disenchanted with the mainline church he had been attending, so he began having his own Bible studies with a few of his friends. Before long, attendance had grown to 15, and Campbell was encouraged to go out recruiting others for their group. Soon he had become a traveling preacher, his unique ideology being a homeless, penniless, and celibate ministry of faith. Others who wanted to go preaching also would do so under Campbell's tutelage. As the preachers became trained, they spread out and an organization emerged to manage the affairs of the budding ministry.

However, this not so distant history is never mentioned among the members. Some time after his organization had begun growing rapidly, it was discovered that Campbell had been having affairs with many of his female converts, so the senior members of the ministry ousted him from his position and expelled him from the organization – on the pretext that he had become influenced by wrong doctrine. To distance themselves from the shameful reputation of their founder, the new leadership decided never to mention his name again.

The sect continued to grow. Today small congregations have been established throughout most of the countries of the world. The group continues to claim a ministry of homeless, penniless, celibate ministers, called servants and handmaidens. Among the lay membership there is such confidence in the ministry that they normally render them unquestioning obedience, their lifelong commitment to their ministry an indication of their worthiness. But then, occasionally, their policy and their practice end up on incompatible tangents. This is a story of one such event.

CHAPTER 1

"Your mother's ready and waiting," Mrs. Roxton said when she answered the door.

"How's she been doing?" B.J. asked.

"Not too bad. She got up before anyone else this morning and has been sitting with her shawl on for an hour."

"I guess she wants to get this over with."

"Poor lady," Mrs. Roxton said, and burst into tears. "I just don't know what to say. I'm so sorry for all of you. I just can't imagine ..."

"Don't cry," B.J. said. "We have the very best attorney working for us."

"I know. I'm glad for that."

Edith emerged from the hallway leading to her private sitting room, carrying an overnight bag and purse.

"Good morning, Mom," B.J. greeted her.

"Good morning, dear."

"I see you're ready to go."

"I am. A dreadful day, isn't it?"

"We don't know that yet."

Edith turned to Mrs. Roxton. "You've been so good to me."

"You've been so good to us," Mrs. Roxton said. "But you *are* coming back, aren't you?"

"Oh dear!" Edith sighed. "I don't know what to plan on these days."

Mrs. Roxton hugged her. "Edith, you'll be fine. We'll be praying for you all the time you're gone, and you'll come back here to us. Remember, we need you, and the children need you. Their nanny is as important to them as their mother and father, you know."

"Thank you," Edith replied. "I appreciate that."

B.J. took his mother's overnight bag and helped her down the steps to his waiting car. For the first time he thought his mother looked old. She was still in her late fifties, but she was becoming stooped and weary looking, especially with the shawl pulled over her shoulders that way. He wanted to cry for what she was about to witness, but he knew he had to be strong for her sake.

"You've got a new car," Edith remarked as she stepped onto the elegantly bricked circular driveway.

"Well, new to me," B.J. agreed. *But it looks like a piece of junk sitting in front of this mansion*, he thought.

"Nice," Edith confirmed.

She was quiet while B.J. made his way out of La Cañada and onto the freeway, headed for Bakersfield. Finally she spoke. "What do you suppose they'll do with her?"

"I have no idea what to expect," B.J. replied. "She doesn't look like a killer to me, and I'm sure she doesn't look like a killer to anyone else."

There was a long silence.

"Can they execute her?" Edith asked.

"No."

"How do you know?"

"She didn't kill anyone," B.J. reminded her.

"But she shot someone."

"You can't execute someone unless there's a dead body."

"Oh," Edith sighed. "I didn't know that. That's good."

B.J. had reminded her of that dozens of times.

"How long will she be in prison?" Edith asked.

"Let's plan on her not going to prison at all."

"I can't plan on that."

"Why not?"

"I've been disappointed too many times in my lifetime."

"I know." B.J. reached over and held her hand. "I'm sorry."

"It's okay," Edith assured him. "Somehow I've gotten through it."

"I'm still sorry for my part in it all. You're the world's best mother."

"You're the world's best son," Edith said, looking at him.

"Oh no."

"Oh yes. I'd have starved to death if it hadn't been for you."

"Mom, I don't want to talk about that."

"It's true. I would *never* forget that."

B.J. couldn't say a word. A huge knot in his throat made it impossible. He gently squeezed her hand, glanced at her, and saw just a hint of a smile on her weary face, and he felt relieved.

"Mom," he finally said. "Did you ever wish you could have your childhood back again?"

Edith looked at him, startled, then replied, "It's too late to think of that now." Then her mind wandered as she watched the traffic on the highway.

Edith had been a much loved and very special child. She was born in the Nevada ranching community of Gardnerville, the only child of her fortyish parents, Jack and Bessie Mercer. She was also the first child born to members of the Way in Nevada – the Way being the somewhat obscure religious sect that had recently made its way into Nevada looking for converts. Aside from that, she was just plain beautiful, with her pretty blue eyes and strawberry blond hair.

Jack and Bessie had been married after World War II had ended. Jack was from Susanville in Northern California, and Bessie was a Voigt from Bishop in the Owens Valley – solid ranching stock from the desert east of the Sierra Nevada. Gardnerville was about halfway between Susanville and Bishop, so Jack took a job there managing a ranch for an aging ranch owner. The job came with a comfortable house, which became Edith's home until she was married.

Edith spent her childhood raising her dolls in an elaborate playhouse constructed by doting Jack, and was constantly attended by her faithful dog Sammy. Together they wandered the cow trails with as many dolls as her carriage would hold, and they contemplated the wonders of nature and the majesty of Job's Peak. Aside from her usual routine with Sammy and the dolls, she looked forward to the twice weekly forty-five mile treks to the Guerra's house in Stagecoach. It was there that a dozen members of the Way routinely gathered for Thursday evening worship and Sunday fellowship.

The other event she always looked forward to was a visit from the servants – usually for a week at a time. Edith understood that the servants were *God's* servants, and the most important people in the world. She was always given a list of *dos and don'ts* before they arrived, but Edith never made any behavioral mistakes while they were there. In fact, one servant, Bart Stanley, took a particular liking to her. He complimented her on her fine manners, her long dresses, and her long hair. It was probably these virtues that prompted Bart to allow her to confess at age eight, and subsequently be baptized in the Carson River at age eleven. Both these events occurred at an unusually early age.

School was somewhat of an unpleasant matter for Edith. She was a model student, but some of her classmates didn't relate well to her. By the third grade a couple of them had decided Edith was weird, but she nevertheless got along well with everyone. Her real problem came in the fifth grade when it became the style at school for the girls to wear pageboy hairstyles. Edith could not have one because Bessie told her, "God doesn't want ladies to touch their hair with scissors." So Edith never asked again.

It was also about that time that Edith's pigtails were replaced with a tidy bun on the back of her head. Her teachers told her it was "stylish", but some of the students thought it was "silly", or "old-lady". Edith, of course, was quite satisfied that it was a very godly hairstyle because it didn't require scissors and it allowed her ears to be visible. Furthermore, all the grown-up women in the Way wore their hair that way. But she was shocked and disappointed when she went that year to their summer retreat in Auburn, California. She heard some of the boys calling her "bun-head" – still, some of the servants complimented her on her new hairdo. That comforted her greatly, because she knew that all she really needed was the approval of the servants.

When the mini-skirt rage came along Bessie had trouble buying appropriate dresses for Edith. She bought the dresses anyway and sewed six or seven inches of contrasting fabric to the hem of each one. Edith understood, but she thought her mother's choice of *coordinating* fabric was horrible. Not surprisingly, only the servants complimented her on the ingenuity of her fashion solution. To avoid any more embarrassment concerning her dresses, she learned to sew herself so she'd not have to wear any more of her mother's *botch jobs*.

It was at the Auburn retreat when she was twelve that she met a boy she'd never seen before. She thought he was gorgeous, and the fact that he was Indian was no small part of the attraction. His name was

Kumar, and his family had recently moved from India to the Bay Area where both his mother and father were going to practice medicine. Edith was so enchanted by him that she had to tell Bessie about him, and of course Bessie told Jack. All the way home from retreat Jack teased Edith about "cooing for Kumar". Edith reluctantly loved the teasing.

From then on the semi-annual retreats in Auburn became the highlight of Edith's life. Kumar was always there, and they became the best of friends. When Edith was fifteen they began writing letters, and Kumar soon dropped the "Your friend, Kumar" in favor of "Love, Kumar". Edith got a tremendously exciting boost to her dreams about their friendship the day she ventured to tell him, "I'd love to wear a sari like Indian women do."

Kumar laughed. "I'll see that you're able to do that some day."

Oh, the dreams she had of wearing a sari and holding hands with Kumar – somewhere in their future together.

The other teenagers at retreat had become her best friends as well, far ahead of any friends she'd made at school. She felt comfortable participating in the girl talk with those girls because they didn't expect her to indulge in any ungodly activities, especially at retreat. It was at retreat that she got her first instruction on bra size. "Here," one girl told her. "It's easy. You measure yourself around the nipples, and then under the boobs, and subtract that one from the nipple one. The difference will tell you how to decide what cup to wear."

"And here's a secret," another told her. "Check the package. Look for words like *push-up* or *lift* or ... you know, something to push them up so the guys will be sure to notice them. Guys love my boobs. I can see them looking at them all the time."

It wasn't the kind of conversation she could have with one of the servants, but it was so exciting and apparently legitimate because all her girlfriends were delighting in their conversations together. In fact, after retreat she sometimes felt more enlightened about teenage girl concerns than about spiritual things. She just never told her parents that!

After they'd driven in silence for a while, B.J. got his nerve up to ask Edith something he always wanted to know. "Why did you marry Dad?"

"The servants told me to."

"What?"

"Yeah."

"You're kidding?"

"No."

And the knot returned to his throat.

"I know I shouldn't ask you this," he apologized, "but do you ever regret marrying Dad?"

There was a long pause.

"I don't know," she murmured. And her mind wandered again.

Edith had had one very heated romantic day in her life. It was in the summer of 1964 at Auburn retreat. She had just graduated from high school, and Kumar had finished his second year at university. On the first day of retreat Kumar asked her if she'd like to go for a walk. Once on the street he suddenly stopped walking, took both her hands in his, and very nervously and seriously announced, "Edith, I most sincerely want you to marry me. I am so much in love with you that I want to spend the rest of my life with you. Will you please marry me – maybe in two years when I get my bachelor's degree?"

Edith almost collapsed. "Yes," was all she could say.

"I'm so happy I could scream." Of course he wouldn't scream while they were only a hundred feet from the retreat gate, so they just stood and held hands and stared at each other for what seemed like forever. Then he dropped one of her hands and said, "Shall we walk on some more?"

"I feel faint," Edith said. "Can we go back and sit on one of the benches again?"

So they did.

Before the retreat was over, everyone had heard about the proposal. Edith knew exactly how that happened. Kumar had told no one, but Edith felt a responsibility to tell her mother. And so the news got around to everyone.

On the second last day of retreat Kumar said to Edith, "Can you meet me this evening after bedtime snacks, over beside the kitchen building, and I'll kiss you before we have to go home."

"Okay." Edith was beaming.

"Don't forget. I'll be waiting."

"I won't forget. I promise." How could she forget? She'd never done anything more than sneak to hold his hand. The prospect of kissing him made her head spin, and she could think of nothing else until the time came.

After most people had retired to the dorms that night, Edith sneaked around the corner of the kitchen building and there was Kumar, waiting for her. She ran to him and he reached out his arms to her and leaned down to kiss her. Then he stopped. "Here comes Bart," he whispered. "Quick, we have to hide."

He pulled her behind the chimney with him, and she squeezed in as tightly as she could to make sure Bart wouldn't see her. Kumar had his arms around her, and she smelled his cologne and felt the strength of his arms around her – and the pressure of her breasts against his chest sent heat flooding through her body. She felt weak in her knees. His lips were hot. She had not expected it, but he was using his tongue, and she trembled.

She had no idea how long their kiss lasted. Then he was whispering in her ear, "Maybe we better not get caught doing any more of this tonight." She felt a stiff protrusion against her abdomen and realized ... well, she was astonished that an erection could occur so *easily* and be so *enormous*. She was breathless with the discovery, and all she could answer was, "Maybe so."

"See you tomorrow," Kumar whispered.

"Yeah." And she ran off to the girls' dormitory ... tripped and almost fell getting through the door.

She hardly slept that night. She relived every second of their encounter behind the chimney. She savored his smell, his strong arms and body, all night. And his whisper echoed in her whole being. She tossed and turned, and her erotic imaginings shocked her, but she had no will whatsoever to stifle them. Once during the night she woke and found herself tangled in her blankets, hugging her pillow, and glad the lights were out and everyone else in the dorm was asleep.

She wondered until morning what she was going to do when she saw Kumar again. She felt like ravishing him, but she knew she couldn't do that on the retreat grounds. She even wondered how she was going to live the rest of her life in this sudden new state of excitement.

But next morning was just like all the other mornings. She and Kumar met, even held hands while waiting for breakfast to be served. It was like any other day at retreat, except for how she felt inside.

As Kumar was leaving that afternoon, he told her, "I'm getting a car this summer, so I'll be able to come and see you in Nevada."

"That'll be good," Edith sighed.

It was less than two weeks later that Bart Stanley drove into the Mercer's yard in Nevada. Edith had always been excited to see the servants coming to their house, but this time she was worried. *Bart must have seen me kissing Kumar,* she was convinced.

Bessie invited Bart in, and apologized that Jack was out working.

"That's okay," Bart said. "This doesn't really concern Jack, I guess."

"What's it about?"

"I hear that you, Edith, are planning to marry that Indian boy," Bart began.

Edith nodded yes.

"We can't have this," Bart declared. "This is not acceptable to the Lord."

Edith said nothing.

"But he's a lovely boy," Bessie protested.

"He *is* a lovely boy," Bart agreed. "It has nothing to do with whether he's a lovely boy or not. He's black, and black and white don't mix."

"I thought he was Indian," Bessie said.

"All the same," Bart said. "God did not put different races on the earth for them to mix."

"I didn't know that," Bessie said.

"It's easy to know," Bart continued. "You've never seen robins mating with blue jays. And you've never seen crows mating with swans. This is how we know that blacks and whites cannot mix."

"Isn't Kumar's uncle married to a white woman?" Bessie asked.

"Yes, and that's an abomination. That should never have been. Nothing good will ever come of that marriage. This is what happens when people do not talk to the servants before they decide who they're going to marry."

"I want to marry Kumar," Edith blurted.

"No you don't," Bart corrected. "You realize you'd not even be able to go into a restaurant in Nevada with him. He's black. You know it's illegal."

"Not anymore," Edith timidly protested. "The Supreme Court declared that law unconstitutional last year."

Bessie was impressed with Edith's learnèd pronouncement, and looked anxiously at Bart.

"Shame!" Bart replied. "The Supreme Court is going to ruin this country with its ungodly rulings. This is just another sign that the last days are upon us. And we cannot depend on the Supreme Court to uphold God's law."

Bessie and Edith stared at him, but said nothing.

"But I have someone in mind for you," Bart continued. "There's a young man in the Bay Area that would be a perfect husband for you. His name is Bernie Kite. He has a good education and a good job, and his parents are very faithful followers of the Way. I'm going to suggest that you marry him. Besides, he has a job and could support you. The Indian only wants to go to school."

"I don't know that guy Bernie," Edith whimpered.

"I'll tell him to introduce himself," Bart promised.

Edith was stunned – and afraid.

Bart stayed for dinner, and talked mostly to Jack. He left shortly after dinner, and Edith fled to her room to cry.

Bessie and Jack followed her to comfort her.

"My best advice to you is to wait and see what happens," Jack concluded after a long talk. "You may never hear anything from this Kite fellow anyway."

"We have to take the servants' advice," Bessie explained. "Especially about marriage. They know things we don't know."

"Like what?" Edith asked.

"Now don't be doubting," Bessie chided. "You know what can happen when we don't obey the servants."

Edith sat silent, and refused to discuss it any more.

When her parents left the room, she closed the door and cried herself to sleep.

"Mom," B.J. interrupted her thoughts again. "You were pretty. You could have had any guy you wanted."

"It's okay," Edith assured him. "I have you and Amber now. That's all I want any more."

B.J. decided he'd asked enough questions for that day. He was afraid he'd overload himself with sadness and that would not do, considering the task ahead of them.

CHAPTER 2

It was Edith who broke the silence next – just as they were descending the Grapevine into the San Joaquin Valley. "I don't think Amber did it," she said.

"Why not?" B.J. asked.

"According to Rocky, Orville said it was Tina Malek."

"Was Rocky there?"

"Yes. He's a servant, you know."

"I can't see him being a servant."

"He's been one for four years now."

B.J. didn't comment.

Stone Lee, or Rocky as his childhood friends called him, went into the service in 1999 at the age of twenty-two. The *service*, to members of the Way, meant the *ministry*. Stone and B.J. had grown up together in the Bay Area and had turned out to be the *bad boy* teens of the Way community in Northern California. Stone, however, continued to go to assembly after B.J. dropped out, and they drifted apart. They hadn't seen each other since then.

"I went to retreat in Poppy Hill after this happened," Edith continued. "The only person who would speak to me was Rocky."

"Why would no one speak to you?" B.J. wondered.

"People were told not to discuss it."

"But didn't people have anything else to say to you? They didn't have to talk about Amber."

"Oh, I don't know, B.J. You know what people are like."

"I know what people in the Way are like," B.J. replied. "They only talk to people they are allowed to talk to."

"You're being hard on them."

"What about all the people you've been friends with for fifty years? Did any of them speak to you?"

There was a long silence. "Oh yes. They all said hello to me."

"But no one really had a conversation with you."

"No, B.J.," Edith protested. "They weren't supposed to be discussing this."

"Mom, I'm going to explain something to you. The only prohibition on people talking to people is for those who are going to testify in court. It's perfectly legal for everyone else to have any conversation they want with you – even about Amber if you wanted to talk about her."

"B.J.! Did you not read the letter Ted van de Kamp sent to everyone?"

"I threw it in the trash."

Christ's Way in California
June 20, 2003

My Dear Friends in the Way,

I've been asked by Mark Volpe to prepare instructions for you with respect to the mishap that occurred this summer in Poppy Hill. As you know, it is not acceptable before God for you, who are destined to judge the angels, to speak of the sins of your brethren to the law. (Cor.6:1-8) However, we have been put in the position where the state will be demanding that some of us answer questions about this mishap, and this brings much sorrow to God's servants and handmaidens when God's children are found in such a situation. In your grief, the servants feel the following godly instructions will be a comfort to all of you to abide by.

Firstly, no one should mention this mishap or discuss it. The authorities in their wisdom have advised everyone they have spoken with to refrain from speaking about these events. We are pleased about that, and want to impress it upon everyone's conscience that this matter should not be mentioned among us – and to concentrate on lovely things and good reports. (Phil.4:8) This will not be very difficult for us if we prepare our spirits for our special days of retreat, which are now less than two weeks away. This will make our days together more peaceful and profitable.

Secondly, we urge everyone who is called upon to speak to the authorities to be mindful of Jesus' refusal to speak before a worldly court. (Jn.19:90) And those of you who are compelled to speak, may it be with honesty and sincerity. We are above all concerned that God's Way will be appropriately reflected by His people to the rest of the world. Remember, we are the only Bible this sinful world will ever read. It is our calling in Christ to be a witness of His spirit in us in all we say and do. We trust this will be our portion in this difficult time as it is in all other times.

Since this letter is not being mailed to households where there are unsaved spouses, the bishops may feel free to give copies to the saved spouse when he/she comes to assembly this week.

Your servant through His mercy
Ted van de Kamp

"Why do the servants get so paranoid about things?" B.J. asked.

"Well, I suppose they just want to be safe, so they just made it so that no one would say anything."

"That makes me angry," B.J. fumed.

"B.J., I don't blame people for not speaking to me. This is the worst thing that has ever happened among the servants – in the Way, anywhere in the world. No one will ever forget this."

"The worst?"

"Yes. Who ever heard of someone getting shot at retreat? Who ever heard of one of the Way friends anywhere shooting anyone? Especially one servant shooting another. What will the rest of the world think of us?"

"You know, Mom, everything that happens at retreat is *not* totally above board."

"Yes, I know that. Kids embarrass their parents all the time with their antics, but for a servant to do something wrong, and such a thing as this! This is unthinkable, terribly unthinkable."

"*Terrible things* is nothing new," B.J. explained. "Why do you suppose Howard Barnes disappeared? And Scott Zinc, and Trent Hansen, and Aaron Finkelstein, and Connie Riggs, and Vince Ho. All those servants disappeared in the last couple of years. No one mentions them any more."

"Servants have a very difficult life," Edith argued. "They leave when their health doesn't allow them to carry on. Anyway, Aaron Finkelstein was a homosexual."

"No. Aaron was *not* a homosexual."

"Well, that's what the servants said. What am I supposed to believe?"

"I think you're going to find some new things to believe."

"Oh dear!" Edith sighed.

"Are you sure you're up to this?"

"I have no choice. It's the only thing I can do for Amber."

"And I'm with you."

"I'm so glad."

"Do you suppose people are going to be mad at us?"

"We don't have to talk to anyone."

"Stay with me, okay."

"I'll be there," B.J. promised.

The unfortunate event they were talking about was the late night shooting of Orville Voigt in Poppy Hill, the site of the semi-annual Way retreats in Southern California. Edith's daughter, Amber, was going on trial for attempted murder. For Edith, there were several distressing aspects of this case, not the least of them that it was bringing shameful publicity on the Way, and that it was her daughter who was being accused of pulling the trigger.

The other distressing aspect was that Orville Voigt was Amber's cousin, and B.J.'s as well, of course. The Mercers from Nevada and the Voigts from Bishop had for three generations been touted by the servants as *lights in the desert* east of the Sierras. The fact that Edith *Mercer* had married Bernie Kite did not help things – everyone knew that Edith's mother had been a Voigt. Bart Stanley, the servant who so admired Edith as a small girl, was still singing Edith's praises in his old age, so everyone in California knew her name and family history. So far Bart had been able to point out her virtues in every disaster that befell her, but she couldn't imagine how he could save her reputation in this one.

Yes, Edith had married Bernie as Bart had advised. But she really was never in love with Bernie. Only days after Bart had told Edith not to marry Kumar, Bernie showed up at assembly in Stagecoach with a shiny new sports car. After the service, he asked her if he could give her a ride home, and she accepted. It was a 45-mile ride, so they had some time to talk.

"Edith, I have a question," Bernie asked as they were leaving the Guerras' yard.

"Yes?"

"I was wondering if you'd marry me."

"Well, I could think about that."

"You see, if you'll marry me, then I'll go with you," he explained. "I don't want to waste my time dating someone who isn't going to marry me."

"Okay, I'll marry you."

"Bart recommended you."

"And Bart recommended you," Edith echoed.

"So we should be good for each other," he concluded. Then he listed his qualifications. "I graduated from high school too. Not just a normal high school, you see. It's a special one for kids who aren't going through the usual schools. They're more mature. They call the diploma *G.E.D.* I think it's better than a usual diploma because you have to be more mature to go to those schools."

Edith looked at him in disbelief, and thought, *Kumar's going to be a doctor.*

"We'll have to get married before New Years," Bernie explained.

It was July, and Edith had never met him before. She wanted some time to get to know him. "So soon?"

"Yeah. Let me ask, have you earned any money yet this year?"

"No. I just graduated from high school."

"Good," he smiled. "Then don't work between now and then, so I can claim you for an income tax deduction for this year."

Whatever, Edith decided.

And Bernie talked on while Edith listened. She couldn't think of anything to say, and he had lots to say, so he wasted no time.

When they pulled into the Mercer's yard in Gardnerville, he held up his left hand and extended his index and middle fingers together.

"Here," he instructed. "Wrap your fingers around this." She wrapped her fingers around his two extended fingers. "Big, long, fat fingers, huh?"

"Yes, they are," Edith stammered.

"Now this," he said, smiling and pulling her fingers back and forth on his own fingers. "This is what you'll be getting when we're married."

She stared at him.

He squeezed her fingers harder and began shoving the extended fingers more aggressively into her hand. She suddenly figured out what he was suggesting, and immediately pulled her hand away.

"You'll love it," he said, opening the door. "Let's go inside and see how much longer it takes your parents to get home than it took us."

They did get married before the end of the year. Bart Stanley took time out from his schedule to attend their wedding on the 29th of December. On Bart's advice, the wedding was held at Bernie's home in Richmond because Bart believed a California marriage would appear to be more respectable than a Nevada marriage. And Bart was very pleased.

When B.J. parked the car at the Bakersfield courthouse that morning, Edith turned to him and said, "I'm just so pleased that you're going to assembly again."

B.J. made a pained face. "I have to talk to you about that," he said, but did not elaborate.

CHAPTER 3

When it was learned that Orville Voigt was the servant who had been shot in Poppy Hill, most Way members thought it was just a terrible tragedy. They poured sympathy upon him and his parents and the rest of the servants alike. What was disconcerting was that Amber, a young handmaiden, was the suspect, and this incident exposed them to public scrutiny – something they avoided and believed they did not deserve.

But B.J. and Orville had a history. Being cousins, they'd visited each other for a week at a time on summer vacations. Orville would go to San José, the big city in the Bay Area; and B.J. would go to Bishop, the Mule Capital of the World. B.J. enjoyed the wide open desert spaces, and the much more relaxed discipline of Orville's parents. Orville was two years younger than B.J., but he had a brother, Oliver, who was seven years older than Orville. The things B.J. and Orville learned from Oliver were fascinating, to say the least. Riding horses and catching rattle snakes made great stories for B.J. to share with his friends back in the city.

Oliver was their hero because he had a driver license already, and B.J. and Orville always begged to go with him. The most memorable event was the day Oliver took them to the hot springs in the mountains. He made the mistake of announcing that he was going to get out of the heat by driving up in the mountains where it was cooler. At first he had refused to take B.J. and Orville with him, but his mother prevailed upon him and he relented.

Oliver put the younger boys in the back seat of his old car and began to lecture them the minute he drove off. "Now you two listen to me," he said. "I'm going to pick up a girl, and you two aren't going to tell anyone about it. You're not going to tell anyone where we went, or what we did, or anything. Make something up, but if I hear you've said anything about this I'll make you pay for it, guaranteed."

"We won't say anything," Orville promised.

"Neither will I," B.J. agreed.

"And another thing," Oliver continued. "When we get there, I want you two to get lost. Disappear. Go somewhere where I can't see you and don't come back for two hours."

"I don't have a watch," Orville protested.

"Here," Oliver said, pulling off his own. "Take mine, and don't you dare show up for two hours, and don't lose my watch either."

"Okay."

Oliver picked the girl up at the pool hall behind one of the town's service stations, and she was a sight to behold. B.J.'s and Orville's eyes literally popped. She was wearing a deep scoop halter top, short shorts, and flip-flops – nothing more. Her breasts were popping out of her top, and the boys in the back seat were speechless. Oliver didn't introduce her.

She slid over close to Oliver and began massaging his neck as he drove off. It wasn't long before she began kissing his neck, and between the seats B.J. and Orville could see her other hand sliding along Oliver's leg. B.J. and Orville were transfixed.

When they arrived at the hot springs, Oliver pulled a blanket from the trunk and said, "Beat it," and B.J. and Orville ran off.

"I want to watch them," Orville said.

"You'll get caught," B.J. warned.

"Heck no. Just keep quiet and we'll see what they do."

"Don't you think we should do what he told us?"

"We can't go anywhere," Orville explained. "I'm scared of the forest. We'll get lost. Anyway, I want to see what they do." So the two of them found a place to hide – and they watched.

Oliver spread the blanket on the ground and he and the girl hurriedly undressed and slowly edged, naked, into the hot water.

"Oh my god," Orville whispered, and B.J. snickered.

"You shouldn't say 'Oh my god,'" B.J. reminded him.

When Oliver and the girl started playing around in the pond, Orville squeaked, "Oh my god." And B.J. snickered again.

When they got out of the water, and Oliver appeared enormously excited, Orville murmured, "Oh my god! Look."

When the girl sat on Oliver's lap, Orville said, "Oh my god," again – louder that time.

"Be quiet or we'll get caught," B.J. said. "And don't say that again."

"Okay." Then he fell over and snapped a small branch off a tree.

"We gotta get out of here," B.J. said. "You're gonna get us in trouble."

"I don't want to get lost in the forest," Orville whined.

"Well then you'll just have to sit still and wait."

"I can't. I have to go to the bathroom."

"Then turn around and pee, but don't make a noise."

"I have to go number two and I can't do that here," Orville complained.

"You don't have to make a noise."

"I don't want you looking at me."

"I won't look," B.J. assured him.

"But I have no toilet paper."

"Then you'll have to hold it."

"Okay."

But it wasn't long before Orville decided he could hold it no longer, and raced out of the trees toward Oliver. "Oliver," he yelled. "I have to go home real fast. I have to go to the bathroom."

The girl grabbed her clothes and ran off into the trees and Oliver grabbed his jeans and covered himself. "I told you to get lost," he yelled.

The party, of course, was over, and the girl wouldn't come out from the trees.

"Get in the car," Oliver yelled, and went to find the girl. After a while he returned with her. She was sobbing while getting into the car. She covered her face and sat still the whole way home. When they got into town, Oliver let her out on the sidewalk and she ran off down a side street. Needless to say there were no more afternoon rides in the car with Oliver.

Nothing was said about the incident until they went to bed that night.

"I can hardly wait to do things like that with a girl," Orville confessed after the light was out.

"They shouldn't be doing that," B.J. said.

"I think they do it all the time," Orville continued. "Oliver talks about it all the time with his friends – they're all big teenagers. And the girls always want it really bad, they say."

"They might get caught."

"How?"

"Girls have babies, you know," B.J. explained. "And everybody knows how they get them."

"I know," Orville agreed. "But that's their problem."

B.J. didn't know what to say – but he decided that Oliver and Orville were more reckless than prudent.

Before the next summer came around, things at home had changed dramatically for B.J. and he was never able to go back to Bishop for vacation. But he did get news. The following summer he heard that Oliver married his pregnant girlfriend two weeks after high school graduation. When the wedding picture arrived at B.J.'s family that fall it was obvious that Oliver had married someone other than the girl he'd cavorted naked with the previous summer.

Later, when Orville was fifteen, he confessed at summer retreat; so B.J. expected that would change Orville's plans for what he'd be doing with girls. But by then B.J. himself had stopped going to weekly assembly and having anything to do with the Way friends, so he didn't get to discuss Orville's conversion with him.

It was another three years later, after B.J. had moved to Los Angeles, that he and Orville got together again. Orville was going to college in Los Angeles, so they got a small apartment together. For the first couple of months Orville's life revolved around his studies and assembly and Sunday fellowship. Then one evening he said to B.J., "I'm really bored. I have to meet some girls."

"Have you not met any at assembly and fellowship?" B.J. queried.

"No. I saw one at a gospel service, but she was so snotty her nose was dripping."

"Rough, isn't it?"

"Where do you find girls?" Orville asked.

B.J. didn't answer.

"Come on, B.J., I know you see girls because you're out almost every night of the week."

"Yeah, I meet girls," B.J. said.

"Where?"

"Go to the gym," B.J. said. "There are lots of girls there – good looking ones too."

"In shape, too, I bet," Oliver mused.

"You got it."

"Take me there. I also wouldn't mind being as buff as you are."

B.J. laughed.

"I mean it," Oliver said. "Are you on steroids or are you just a big pretty boy?"

"Nothing but hard work," B.J. assured him. "I guess now that you're in the city you'll not be able to keep fit like you did in Bishop."

"Anything to meet girls," Orville pointed out.

Orville did have girls back in Bishop – lots of them. Shortly after he'd moved in with B.J. he confided that he was glad to get out of Bishop. "Too many girls," he confessed. "I was afraid of getting in trouble."

"Seems like you survived better than Oliver did," B.J. guessed.

"Oliver was so stupid. He should have used condoms."

"So I suppose you did, huh?"

"You bet your ass," Orville assured him.

So much for being a good little Way boy, B.J. thought.

And Orville found girls in Los Angeles. He'd always been muscular and athletic, but with weight training he shaped up like a bodybuilder, restyled his reddish-blond hair, and grew an attractive goatee. By the end of the first semester he was having as many as five dates a week, and he saw less and less of B.J. But by the end of the second semester he was in serious trouble.

"What's wrong with you?" B.J. asked one afternoon.

"I'm really up a creek," Orville explained. "This girl I dated a couple of times tells me she's having my baby."

"I thought you used condoms."

"She told me one must have busted."

"Have you decided what to do?"

"No. But I certainly don't want to marry her."

"Well, let me know if there's something I can do for you."

"Why me?" Orville moaned. "You're out chasing it every night of the week all year and nothing happens. How do you get off with that?"

"First of all, I'm not chasing it. And secondly, I don't exactly fuck them."

Orville studied him. "What do you do every night of the week?"

"I work," B.J. said.

"Yeah! What do you work at?"

"Odd jobs."

"I thought you worked at the gym."

"Part time," B.J. said, and grabbed his gym bag and left.

The baby problem didn't get resolved for many months. The girl wanted Orville to marry her, but he refused. She had an attorney write him a letter and advise him of his responsibilities with respect to her pregnancy and the expected child. Orville had an attorney write her a letter advising her that Orville was not going to accept any responsibility until it was confirmed through DNA testing that he was indeed the father of the child. And then the child was born.

In late September Orville's attorney handed him a copy of the DNA report that confirmed there was no possibility that he could be the father of the child, so *that* matter was closed.

But another matter had arisen. Orville was suffering deeply from the guilt associated with his dropping out of the Way to carry on with his promiscuous lifestyle. He finally decided that, as hard as it was going to be on him, he was going to straighten up his life and confess again and *get saved* again. He contacted the local servants and asked where they were having gospel services – he was interested in returning to the Way.

After a couple of weeks he came home from gospel service and announced to B.J., "I've re-confessed."

"Good for you," B.J. said.

"You should confess too, I think."

"No. I can't."

"Why not?"

"I have too much to give up right now."

Orville didn't ask what that might be. "Well, I've discovered I have more to give up than I expected."

"How's that?"

"After I confessed tonight I was talking to the servants, and Paul Patten wanted to know if I'd ever fornicated."

"And you said?"

"I said yes, of course. You can't lie to a servant."

"I'm sure a lot of people have."

"Well, I'm not about to do that right now."

"So what difference?"

"Now I can't get married," Orville explained. "Paul told me I've already been joined to a woman so now I can't marry anyone but her."

"*Her?*" B.J. mocked. "Isn't it more like *them?*"

"Come on, B.J. I have to go into the service now."

"For real?"

"Yeah. According to Paul, if you've fornicated and then don't want to marry the girl you can't marry anyone else. The only option left is to be a servant. I don't want to be a preacher. Do you suppose maybe, if I explain it to him, that if I got married, an exception could be made ... you know ... I used a condom? Suppose that would count as *not joining* ..."

"Good luck with that," B.J. snickered.

"You're no help at all."

Two years later Orville announced he was dropping out of college and going in the service. B.J. had no real news of him again until he was shot.

CHAPTER 4

When they entered the courthouse, B.J. surprised Edith by announcing that she'd have to go into the courtroom by herself. "Oh my!" she stuttered.

"Because *I* may have to testify," B.J. explained.

"Really?"

"Yes."

"I hope they don't want to ask me anything."

"Don't worry. You'd know by now if they wanted you to testify. But you won't be alone. Someone else is going to come and stay with you for a while."

"Who?"

"Hattie Burk," B.J. said. "She promised me she'd be here."

"Whatever for?"

"She just wanted to make sure you weren't alone. And she likes you and Amber very much, you know."

Edith smiled. "I like her. You'll be here when I come out?"

"Oh yes, I'll be here, or outside in my car."

"Okay."

Edith found herself a seat in the front row at one end of the room and got comfortable. It was very quiet – a very somber atmosphere – and a couple of uniformed officers were busying themselves about the room. What appeared to be secretaries came in and began setting up at various desks, and someone tapped a microphone somewhere and got the required boom from the speakers.

The door opened behind her, and in came a couple of Way friends from Bakersfield and one of the servants. She thought they glanced her way then turned and took seats at the opposite end of the room. A man who looked like an attorney came in with a lady who looked like his secretary, and they went to one of the desks in front of the judge's bench and began opening brief cases and laptops.

Then Hattie appeared. Edith was greatly relieved.

Hattie was the oldest handmaiden in California. Edith remembered Hattie saying once at retreat that she'd been in the service for 60 years, yet there she came very gingerly approaching Edith, and threw a hug around her neck. "My dear Edith. I'm so glad to see you."

"I'm glad to see you too," Edith smiled. "Isn't this terrible?"

"Hush, hush now." Hattie whispered as she settled herself into the seat beside Edith. "We're just going to hold each other's hands and something good will happen. Life just has its little detours from time to time."

Edith was startled at her positiveness. "You think so?"

"Of course, dear. I just knew I had to come here to tell you that."

Edith noticed that the servant and friends at the other end of the room were watching them. "You're so thoughtful," she said. "I was feeling quite alone here by myself."

"Of course," Hattie agreed. "Do you know why?"

"Well, ..."

"See those guys over there – looking at us. I knew someone would come here and do that, so I intentionally came here to sit beside you. It's a terrible thing that brothers and sisters in Christ would just sit there and look at you."

"I think I can understand ..."

"But don't worry about it," Hattie interrupted. "I'm not supposed to be here myself." She chuckled.

"No?"

"I told Uncle Mark that I was coming here today, and he told me to stay away." She tittered to herself. "Wait until he hears that I came here anyway."

"Are you going to be in trouble?"

"Let me tell you, dear, there's not much they can do with a 93-year old lady. I was in the service for at least ten years before Uncle Mark was even born."

"But aren't you supposed to be in Poppy Hill?"

"Of course," Hattie agreed. "But I just told my companion, Tiffany, that I had to be here and that she was going to have to drive me."

"Tiffany's with you?"

"Yes. She decided to visit a library."

Edith smiled, thinking, *That's why everyone's always thought Hattie was an old rebel.*

"You see, it's much easier for me to get forgiveness than it is for Tiffany," Hattie continued. "I'm old enough to be her great grandmother."

"Aren't you going to be missed in Poppy Hill?"

"Only at roll call."

"You're a hot ticket, Hattie."

"It's also much easier to get forgiveness than it is to get permission. I learned that a long time ago."

Hattie was a remarkable lady. For what seemed like decades she'd been the shrunken, wrinkled, and wobbly old handmaiden who wore funny clothes. She always wore black stockings and lace-up boots; and her dresses were all black, navy blue, dark brown, or dark green with white bib-like collars and fringes of white lace around the neck. The children loved her because she'd pretend to chase them at retreat time, and when she'd catch them she'd give them candy and tell them how well they were behaving at retreat.

The kids even liked her preaching. She frequently told stories about what happened to her when she was small, and they were constantly amused when she mentioned spats she had with her siblings and school mates – especially when she was getting the best of guys much bigger than she. Everyone had a memory of some humorous tale Hattie had shared.

People also whispered about Hattie. She apparently had her differences with Uncle Floyd, the former head servant for California, but she never got sent home as so many expected. Uncle Floyd frequently referred to her as "that woman!" when he was frustrated about something, but Hattie held on to her status as handmaiden. It was always a matter of great speculation what she could have done to upset Uncle Floyd, but no one ever found out.

"Amber was the sweetest little girl," Hattie told Edith. "I can't tell you how pleased I was to have her as my companion the first year she was in the service."

"Thank you," Edith smiled. It made Edith feel good to hear such a pronouncement at such a time.

"And then when she was assigned to be with me again for a whole second year, it was just wonderful. She was everything we'd want a young handmaiden to be. She was quiet, patient, and so accepting of all the direction given her. I used to tell Uncle Floyd that Amber was a little gem, and he was really pleased to hear that about her."

"I'm so glad."

"Some young people, when they go into the service, have real problems accepting correction and submitting to their older companions. They just don't want to have their own wills broken, I've been told." She paused. "I never had a companion like that."

"That's good."

There was a long pause, then Hattie said, "I've sometimes wished they'd give all the new handmaidens to me at least for their first year because I could comfort them as they learned how to fit into the new life they'd chosen."

"Your motherly instinct," Edith speculated.

"Edith, you are something!" Hattie smiled. "What a nice compliment for a handmaiden to get! Motherly instinct. Handmaidens should all have that, don't you think?" She looked directly into Edith's eyes.

"Why yes," Edith said. "I think you're right." She almost felt guilty commenting – it never occurred to her that she should have any opinion about how a servant or handmaiden should behave.

A door opened almost in front of them and Amber came in accompanied by a fortyish man Edith recognized as Clay Shipman, Amber's attorney. She'd seen him at retreat a number of times – years ago. Something happened to him, she'd heard, and he stopped coming to assembly. She sensed from conversations that he'd gotten a bad spirit about something and left the Way, but for some reason the Way friends continued to go to him with legal problems. He was supposed to have defended a notorious Chinese criminal and got him off. The trial was on television and people talked about it for a long time. Possibly he just liked being on TV more than being in the Way.

Edith stared, transfixed, at Amber as she went to her seat. Amber smiled and waved, and Edith waved back. Edith felt her heart beat faster as she realized the trial was about to begin.

"There's one handmaiden I think Amber had a difficult time with," Hattie continued, when Amber was comfortably seated.

"Really?"

"Yes. Lois Snyder. Maybe Amber never said anything to you."

"Never a word." Edith shook her head.

"Isn't that like Amber!" Hattie sighed. "Amber never said a word about anyone."

Edith was puzzled. "Is that a good thing?"

"It can be, it can be. But I sometimes think some of these handmaidens would fare better in the service if they were more able to talk to others about their differences."

"You think so?"

"Yes, dear. Some things need to be told, you know."

Edith didn't know what to say.

"Before they get started, I want to tell you something else too," Hattie whispered. "Don't take a word Bart Stanley says about anyone seriously."

Edith was startled.

Hattie smiled, and nodded to indicate her certainty, and said, "He's kind of a mean old man."

Suddenly a uniformed man cried in a loud voice, "All rise. This court is now in session, the Honorable Judge Donna Green presiding."

And the court came to order.

CHAPTER 5

It was the morning after Amber's arrest in Poppy Hill that an anxious young man burst into the law office of Katz, Berry, and Shipman in Santa Monica. "I need to talk to Mr. Shipman," he said. "Right now."

"I'll check and see if he's busy," the secretary said. "May I ask who wants to see him?"

"Yeah, me," he said. "I'm Marty Spinner."

"What is this about?"

"A friend of mine got shot, and he needs a lawyer," he said. "Well, actually, it's my friend who shot him who needs a lawyer."

"Oh," the secretary replied. "Please have a seat and I'll check with him."

"Did you know that Amber Kite shot Orville Voigt?" Marty asked as he sat down in front of Clay's desk.

"What?"

"The night before last, up in Poppy Hill. And Amber is going to need help."

"What happened?"

"I don't know," Marty said. "No one knows. I was just talking to Amber's brother this morning. He was in his car all night in Bakersfield waiting to get into the jail to see her. He said he didn't know what to do next, so I came to see you."

Clay shook his head. "This is pretty bad. I can't imagine what's going on in Poppy Hill right now."

"All the servants and handmaidens were there, preparing the place for retreat. I've heard of a lot of strange things, but never a shooting at a retreat."

"Obviously it was Amber who had the gun," Clay concluded. "Why did she have a gun? Why would a handmaiden have a gun? Why would any servant have a gun, for that matter?"

Marty stared at Clay for a while, then said, "I heard this on the news this morning. That's why I called B.J."

"What did B.J. say?'

"He said he didn't know what to do. I just told him I'd talk to you if he wanted, and he said okay. We didn't know what else to do."

"Tell B.J. to call me."

"Okay. Will do."

Clay smiled. "You're not trying to stir up more shit on the servants, are you?"

"Not this time," Marty replied. "I just always liked Amber and B.J. and I trust you."

"Thanks," Clay said. "I appreciate that."

B.J. had learned about the shooting from Edith the evening before – almost twenty four hours after it occurred. She hadn't read a newspaper, heard a radio, or seen anything on television. Bart Stanley had called her from Poppy Hill.

Bart always showed up when Edith was about to hear bad news. "I have some very bad news for you, Edith. I'm sure it's going to be difficult for you to deal with."

"What is it? What's wrong?"

"Your daughter, Amber, shot Orville Voigt last night."

Edith was shocked speechless, and didn't say a word.

"Are you still there, Edith?"

"Yes."

"I told you Amber shot Orville last night."

"I don't understand."

"But don't worry, she didn't kill him. He's in the hospital in critical condition. That'll comfort you."

"What happened?"

"We're not sure. It was probably after midnight and they were outside. I don't know what her problem was."

"Why did she … … where did she get a gun?"

"Oh, we don't know, Edith. Who knows what was going on with her? But she'll be in desperate trouble now."

Crying silently, she asked him, "What should I do?"

"I don't think there's anything you can do now, Edith. She's safely in jail where she can't harm anyone else. Unfortunately she's really done herself in with this episode. I just thought I'd call you to comfort you in case you didn't know about this."

She hesitated to answer. "Oh, thank you for letting me know."

"Well, I'll say goodnight for now," Bart concluded the conversation.

Edith slowly put the phone down and began to sob loudly.

"What's the problem, dear? Mrs. Roxton asked, rushing into the room.

Edith turned and hugged her, clinging to her for dear life. "Amber shot someone."

"Oh, lord. You poor soul."

"I don't know what to do. I need to talk to B.J."

Mrs. Roxton called B.J. and told him what had just happened, and B.J. was there within an hour. He hugged Edith fiercely, talked to her, and made a couple of telephone calls to find out where Amber was – she was in a jail in Bakersfield.

B.J. couldn't tell his mother anything more than she already knew, of course, so all he could do was promise to look after everything for her. "I'll go up there right now."

"What about Orville?" Edith pleaded. "Is he going to die?"

"I'll see everyone I can and let you know."

Before B.J. had arrived at the house, Mr. Roxton had called in their neighbor, a physician, because Edith had become almost hysterical. He gave them a prescription for Edith, which Mr. Roxton took to the pharmacy. After B.J. had been with Edith for half an hour her medication was beginning to calm her down, and she decided she'd better go to bed and sleep.

B.J. went straight to Bakersfield, but there was one thing he hadn't planned on – no one is allowed to visit people in jail or visit nonfamily members in intensive care in the middle of the night. He was asleep in his car when Marty woke him with his telephone call.

Clay Shipman got another visit about two hours after Marty left his office.

"Good morning," Mark Volpe greeted him.

"Good morning, Mark," Clay replied. "How are you?" *And what is the head servant's involvement in this matter?*

"Oh fine, fine," Mark assured him. "And you and Nancy and the little ones?"

"We're doing well, thank you."

"Glad to hear that."

"What can I do for you today?"

"We've had an accident at Poppy Hill," Mark began. "I don't know whether you've heard about it or not."

"I just learned about it this morning," Clay said.

"I'm here to see if I could have you help me ... or rather, help Lois Snyder, if necessary."

Clay thought for a minute. "I was expecting you to ask for help for Amber Kite."

"Well, no. I don't know what we could do for Amber right now."

"What's Lois' problem?"

"Well, you see, there's no problem right now, but I'm wondering if there becomes a problem whether you would be able to help her."

Clay studied him. *I hardly dare ask what her problem could be.* So rather than ask, he waited.

And Mark continued. "Lois has indicated that she couldn't handle it if she were to be confronted with officials asking her questions. So just in case, it would be good if she had some counsel if she were confronted with that."

"Has she done something that could be considered a crime?"

Mark thought for a minute. "Of course not. But she's very emotionally fragile, you know."

"In an investigation the police are going to want to talk to anyone who has any knowledge of anything that might assist in their determining exactly what happened. They'll want to know all the circumstances. It's necessary."

Mark looked worried.

Clay continued. "I have to tell you, though, I only work with people who are accused of committing crimes; that is, they've broken some criminal law. If she's been drinking beer in the handmaidens' dorm it's probably immoral, but it's certainly not illegal. On the other hand, if she's been molesting someone's children, then that's a crime, and I could help her in that situation."

Mark flushed. "She's not been involved in that, for sure."

"Does she know anything about the Amber-Orville matter? Was she involved in some way? Was she a witness to something?"

There was a long pause. Mark scratched his head, then said in a low voice, "I'm sure she is … has to be. She was seriously distressed this morning, and I didn't dare ask her many questions. I'm really concerned about her … emotionally."

"In any case, I should tell you that I've tentatively accepted to be counsel for Amber, and if Lois had some involvement with that incident, I'd not be able to help Lois. Conflict of interests, you understand."

"I suppose." Mark looked stunned. "Then perhaps I should wait and see if Lois will need any help, and then find someone else to help her."

"There are lots of attorneys who could help her, I'm sure. But if she's just a witness with nothing criminal to hide, she hasn't any good reason to be afraid to testify."

"I'll tell her that. Hopefully it'll calm her down."

CHAPTER 6

Edith and Hattie sat quietly while the trial got underway. Just before the prosecutor began his opening remarks, Hattie nudged Edith and pointed out a group of seven local Way friends that had quietly come into the courtroom and were seated not far from them.

"I'm glad some of them came," Hattie whispered.

Edith nodded.

The prosecutor proceeded to outline for the jury the kind of evidence they could expect him to present, evidence which would allow them to come to a verdict of *guilty* on the charge of attempted murder. "Ladies and gentlemen," he thundered. "You are going to learn that Miss Kite has for years kept notes about those she did not like, and notes about the fate some of them would come to. The unfortunate Mr. Voigt was the second name on her list – written there more than fifteen years ago. There are other names on her list as well, and we can reasonably assume that, should she be allowed to go free, she would also target any one of them next. Miss Kite needs to be kept off the street so she cannot do further harm."

Edith shuddered, and Hattie held her hand.

"The charge of being in possession of an unregistered handgun is, in the state's opinion, not open for debate. Miss Kite has recorded and acknowledged that she was in possession of such a weapon."

When he finished, Hattie turned to Edith and whispered, "Do you believe all that?"

"I don't know," Edith shrugged.

"I don't believe all that," Hattie said. "He's making some of that up, I'm sure."

Edith sighed deeply.

"I wonder what Clay's going to say about her."

Clay, of course, had quite another view of the matter. "Miss Kite was certainly not on a rampage to *get even* with all the people she did not like. As a matter, Miss Kite did not even know who it was she had shot at in the dark after midnight; and when she found out who it was she was devastated – because it was her own second cousin whom she loves dearly."

Edith nodded her head, and Hattie squeezed her hand.

"What you are going to learn is that Miss Kite had a long history of egregiously abusive treatment, both physically and emotionally, within the religious community to which she belonged. And on the night of the incident in question she did the only thing she could to prevent what she believed was an imminent assault on her. She was alone in a dangerous place after midnight, with no security measures whatsoever in place. I will demonstrate for you that the crime rate in these retreat facilities is no less than in the city of Los Angeles – the crime just occurs in the dark, is never reported, is vehemently denied, and when all else fails, is justified in the name of righteousness."

Edith looked at Hattie. Hattie looked startled, and turned to Edith. "How can he say that?"

"I don't know," Edith said. "He must know something we don't know."

"Well I should say!" Hattie studied Clay when he sat down. "And to think he used to be one of us!"

"I know," Edith agreed.

And the prosecution called Orville Voigt.

Meanwhile, B.J. had found a comfortable park bench where he settled down to read a book while he sipped a cup of coffee. When the day heated up he could always find somewhere indoors to read. There were lots of people swarming around, but no one B.J. knew, so he ignored them. He even ignored the media van that drove up and parked barely fifty feet from him. After all, it was a normal day at a busy courthouse.

What he couldn't ignore was the skinny hand that lurched into his line of vision – and belonged to a little old man with horn-rimmed glasses and a dollop of white hair above his forehead. It was none other than Bart Stanley. B.J. hadn't seen him for many years.

"Good morning, B.J.," Bart said.

"Good morning, Bart. Long time no see."

"Yes. I want to tell you how sorry I am for your mother at this time."

"Thank you. I'll tell her."

"Truly difficult for her."

"It's been difficult on all three of us."

"Well, yes," Bart agreed. "But of course Amber knows what she's done, so for sure she's worried about what's ahead for her."

B.J. became suddenly angry. "You have no sympathy for her at all, do you?"

"Well, it's pretty difficult to have sympathy for one who shoots one of God's true servants."

"You think she lost her mind," B.J said, closing his book.

"As the scriptures say: It would be better for her *that a millstone be hanged about* her *neck, and that* she *were drowned in the depth of the sea*, than to hurt one of God's little ones."

"Ah bull," B.J. spat. "I'm not going to have any conversation about Amber with you."

"It's a shame. Your mother is a wonderfully godly woman."

"And you gave her a life of total misery."

Bart stared at him, shocked.

"You told her to marry my father, didn't you?"

"She was going to marry that black Indian." Bart's eyes began to pop. "Would you want a father like that?"

That really took B.J. by surprise. He'd never heard of a *black Indian*.

"Would you like to be a half-breed?"

"My father wasn't so great," B.J. protested. "I'll never forget the day you praised him for whipping me until my leg was bleeding. You're a ..."

Suddenly Bart lurched away, and B.J. was approached from behind by two men, one of them carrying a huge camera on his shoulder. The letters *KGRT* were embroidered onto each man's shirt.

"Excuse me, sir," the man with the microphone said. "Was that man Bart Stanley?"

"Yes," B.J. said, trying to calm his anger.

"How do you know him?"

"He's supposed to be a preacher, but he's made a wreck of our family."

"I'm Jock Miller," the man with the microphone said, extending his hand. "Are you here for the Kite trial?"

"Yes." Then B.J. recognized the newsman. He said, "I'm her brother."

"Do you mind if I ask you some questions, then?"

B.J. hesitated. "They're expecting me to testify."

"I overheard you telling Mr. Stanley that he praised your father for whipping you? Mr. Stanley once told me he believes in non-violence. Can you tell me something about that?"

"No," B.J. replied. "Please, I can't talk about that now."

The raw, stinging memory sent a hot anger running through B.J.'s veins. It was a long time long ago, probably when he was about eleven, that Bart showed up at their door one Saturday morning. B.J. and Amber were normally expected to stay in the house and sit up and listen when their parents were visiting with the servants. But that morning they were asked to go outside and play until Edith called them in for lunch.

Lunch time came, and they were called in. They washed their hands and went directly to the table, Bart said grace, and they began to eat. Very little was being said. Edith looked especially shame-faced, and Bernie was very calm and polite for a change.

B.J. could never remember the conversation that started the incident, but at one point in the discussion around the table Bart said, "Let me think, now, I seem to have lost my train of thought."

"You had a brain fart?" B.J. asked.

Amber snickered, and Edith put a hand on her arm to quiet her.

"You come with me," Bernie said sternly, and grabbed B.J.'s arm and pulled him outside to the back yard.

When the door closed, Bernie pulled off his belt and began slashing at B.J.'s bare legs. B.J. jumped to avoid the swing of the belt, but Bernie got him in a corner between the porch and the wall of the house and whipped him unmercifully – until B.J. fell on the ground.

Bernie stopped. "Get up," he yelled. "Go back to the table and finish your lunch and don't you say a word."

B.J. limped indoors, heaving and sobbing. He sat in his chair and did not move.

"It's time to finish your lunch," Bernie ordered.

B.J. picked up his fork. His hand was shaking and tears fell onto his food.

Amber was sneaking peeks at the red welts on B.J.'s legs. Then she noticed some small drops of blood start to ooze from one of them and she turned the other way and vomited on the floor.

Edith dropped her fork and took Amber to her room; then returned with a cloth and towel to wipe up the floor.

"You're a remarkable father," Bart said when Edith resumed her place at the table.

B.J. trembled and gasped loudly, and felt sick to his stomach.

"This child will learn not to be disrespectful of adults and servants," Bart confirmed.

"I should hope so," Bernie replied. "I *do* try to remember the saying *spare the rod and spoil the child*."

"Yes, it's true," Bart agreed. "Too many men have abandoned their responsibility to keep their houses in order these days. They're afraid of using the rod, unfortunately."

A black Indian? B.J. wondered.

CHAPTER 7

PROSECUTOR: Why were you dressed and outside your dorm after midnight?
ORVILLE: I had to use the restroom, so I got dressed and went out.
PROSECUTOR: You had to go outdoors to a restroom?
ORVILLE: Yes. There are no restrooms in the dorms at our retreat.
PROSECUTOR: So you go to the restroom.
ORVILLE: Yes.
PROSECUTOR: And did you in fact go to the restroom?
ORVILLE: No.
PROSECUTOR: Why did you not go to use the restroom?
There was a lengthy pause.
ORVILLE: I was shot.
PROSECUTOR: Tell the jury what you can remember about that.
ORVILLE: Well, I was going into the fenced yard in front of the restrooms, and as I went through the gate I saw a person move. The next thing I knew I was knocked around and fell down – and there was a loud bang. Maybe a couple of bangs.
PROSECUTOR: And then?
ORVILLE: I thought I heard a woman screaming. I was very confused. I got up and tried to make my way back to my dorm but I didn't make it. I collapsed in front of the door.

CLAY: Mr. Voigt, had you ever previously gone to the restroom at retreat at night?
ORVILLE: Yes, sir.
CLAY: Frequently?

ORVILLE: Frequently.

CLAY: How frequently? Once a night, every second night? On average.

ORVILLE: Probably every second night.

CLAY: To the same restroom, I presume.

ORVILLE: Uh, yes.

CLAY: How many restrooms are there at these retreat facilities?

Orville's face turned red.

ORVILLE: Umm, I think there are two.

CLAY: But you're not sure?

ORVILLE: Well, yes. I'm sure. There are two.

CLAY: I presume one is for men and one is for women. Am I right?

ORVILLE: Yes.

CLAY: Which of these two restrooms is closest to the men's dorm?

ORVILLE: The men's.

CLAY: And which one were you heading to that night?

ORVILLE: Well, uh, it was the women's ... yeah, the women's.

CLAY: And this was the restroom you always went to at night?

ORVILLE: Well ... sometimes.

CLAY: You just told us you always went to the same restroom.

ORVILLE: Well, uh, it would depend, I guess.

CLAY: On what?

ORVILLE: Whether anyone else was there ... maybe.

CLAY: Was there anyone in the men's restroom that night?

ORVILLE: Well, I didn't check.

CLAY: Did you know at the time who shot you?

ORVILLE: I thought it was Tina Malek.

CLAY: Why did you think it was Tina Malek?

ORVILLE: I just thought she'd be there.

CLAY: Had Tina Malek ever been there before at night when you went out to the restroom?

Orville frowned and looked around the courtroom.

ORVILLE: Yes, a few times.

"See," Hattie whispered. "That young man should never have been there. There was no excuse for him being there at all."

Edith was shocked. "What was he doing in the ladies' restroom?"

Hattie twisted her face and looked at Edith as if to say: *You know exactly what he was doing there.*

"I'm sorry this had to happen," Edith murmured. "What a tragedy?"

"I think this is only the beginning," Hattie opined. "Don't be surprised if you hear a lot worse than this."

"You know everything that happened?"

"Oh, no," Hattie smiled. "I've just been around for a long time."

Edith glanced around to see how the others of the Way friends were reacting. All their faces were devoid of emotion. *They're all too embarrassed to look at me*, Edith thought. *Poor Orville – now he looks as bad as Amber. He'll be kicked out of the service for sure now! And I wonder what Uncle Mark will think of us now.*

"The prosecution calls Delbert Caprio"

PROSECUTOR: How do you know the defendant?

DELBERT: I'm a servant, and she's a handmaiden.

PROSECUTOR: Can you tell us what that means to the general public?

DELBERT: A servant is a male minister in our faith, and a handmaiden is a female minister.

PROSECUTOR: So on the evening in question you were sleeping in the same place as was Mr. Voigt.

DELBERT: That's correct.

PROSECUTOR: Tell the jury what occurred that roused you from your sleep that night.

DELBERT: I woke when I heard Orville getting out of his bed and getting dressed. I expected he was going to the restroom, so I turned over and attempted to go back to sleep.

PROSECUTOR: And?

DELBERT: And it wasn't long before I heard what sounded like two shots and a woman kind of screaming, and then it was quiet.

PROSECUTOR: What did you do then?

DELBERT: I got out of bed and went to the door to see what had happened, and just as I opened the door Orville fell on his face – right in front of the door.

PROSECUTOR: Did Mr. Voigt speak to you when he fell down?

DELBERT: I believe I heard him say, "Tina Malek shot me." His voice was very weak, but I'm sure that's what he said.

PROSECUTOR: Did he say anything else?

DELBERT: No. I thought he was unconscious. He was breathing, but I couldn't get him to say anything. I turned on the light inside the door and saw that he was bleeding, so I went for help.

PROSECUTOR: Where did you go for help?

DELBERT: I went to the house where the head servant was sleeping, and I knocked on his door.

PROSECUTOR: Tell us what transpired there.

DELBERT: Well, I had to knock a couple of times, three times actually, because the door was locked. Then one of the handmaidens answered the door and I told her I needed to speak to Uncle Mark because Orville had been shot. She told me to wait a minute and closed the door. And I waited for a while and then she came back out and ran straight to the ladies' dorm without saying anything to me.

PROSECUTOR: Who is Uncle Mark?

DELBERT: That's what we call the head servant. His name is Mark Volpe.

PROSECUTOR: Did you ever get to talk to Mr. Volpe?

DELBERT: Yes. He came out a minute later and he went to see what happened to Orville.

PROSECUTOR: Did you do anything else for Orville?

DELBERT: I told Mark that he had to get Orville to a hospital, and then I checked to see if I could keep Orville from bleeding too much. There was quite a bit of blood on his shirt by then.

PROSECUTOR: Did Mr. Volpe help you with Orville?

DELBERT: No. He left me there and went to get Victor to take Orville to the hospital in his helicopter.

PROSECUTOR: Who is Victor?

DELBERT: He's the owner of the property. He lives in the house where Uncle Mark has his apartment. His name is Victor Bergman.

PROSECUTOR: Did you have any more communication with Orville that night?

DELBERT: Not really. I just stayed with him until they took him in the helicopter to Bakersfield.

CLAY: Were there other servants in the dorm that night besides you and Orville?

DELBERT: Yes.

CLAY: How Many? Can you remember?

DELBERT: I expect about twenty-five.

CLAY: Did you call for any of them to come and help you?

DELBERT: Uh, no. I was kind of panicked.

CLAY: Would that not have been a logical first step?

DELBERT: Maybe. I guess so. But I turned on the light and they were all awake anyway.

CLAY: Who was the handmaiden who answered the door when you went to wake up Mr. Volpe?

DELBERT: Lois Snyder.

CLAY: How long did you wait for Miss Snyder to answer the door – the first time?

DELBERT: Probably four or five minutes. I had to knock three times, I remember.

CLAY: And all she did was close the door and go back upstairs to get Mr. Volpe?

DELBERT: Yes.

CLAY: How long was it before she came out again?

DELBERT: It seemed like ... I don't know. Maybe five more minutes. I'm not good at telling time.

CLAY: How long did it take Mr. Volpe to wake Mr. Bergman?

DELBERT: It was quite a while. It seemed like quite a while anyway.

CLAY: How long did it take to get Mr. Voigt into the helicopter?

DELBERT: It was quite a while. They had to get a big piece of canvas and make a kind of stretcher to carry him on, and they had to lift him into the helicopter. We didn't have a real stretcher to put him on.

CLAY: Did anyone, to your knowledge, call an ambulance?

DELBERT: Not to my knowledge?

CLAY: Did anyone call the police?

DELBERT: Not to my knowledge.

CLAY: Did anyone call anywhere for help?

DELBERT: Yes. Uncle Mark went to the women's dorm and asked Lois Snyder to come back out and help them take Orville to the hospital.

CLAY: Did anyone, to your knowledge, call anywhere for rescue professionals before Mr. Voigt was put in the helicopter?

DELBERT: No. Not to my knowledge.

CLAY: From the time Orville was shot until he was put on the airplane, how much time do you estimate elapsed?

Delbert thought for a minute.

DELBERT: Maybe fifteen minutes. I was afraid they wouldn't get to the hospital fast enough.

What was Lois Snyder doing in Uncle Mark's apartment in the middle of the night? Edith thought. She decided against asking Hattie – Hattie looked distressed.

CHAPTER 8

At the noon recess, a lady stopped Marty as he was leaving the courthouse. "Excuse me, sir. Can I speak to you a minute?"

"Okay." Marty was curious. Not far from her were two men, apparently reporters – one of them had a television camera on his shoulder.

"My name is Frieda Blaze, and I'm a correspondent with the *Los Angeles Times*. I noticed in the courtroom that you were taking a ... highly studious curiosity about the proceedings. Do you mind if I ask you some questions?"

"No. Maybe not."

Suddenly the two men turned and approached them.

"A second until we're ready to tape?" the one with the camera asked Ms. Blaze.

"Sure," Ms. Blaze replied. And to Marty she said, "This is Jock Miller. He's a reporter for KGET here in Bakersfield."

"Oh!" Marty replied.

"I saw you in the courtroom this morning," Ms. Blaze began. "I was wondering if you knew any of the people involved with the Kite case. No one else will talk to me."

"I'm not surprised," Marty said. "These people are pretty secretive."

"I gather that," Mr. Miller said. "I talked to Miss Kite's brother this morning, but he was consumed with some violence involving another pastor against his family, apparently."

"We call our pastors *servants*."

"It was a Mr. Stanley," Mr. Miller said. "Do you know him?"

"Who doesn't know him?" Marty quipped. "Brutal Bart himself!"

"So he has a reputation?" Ms. Blaze asked.

"That he has, indeed!"

"Are you a member of the Way?" Ms. Blaze asked.

Marty hesitated, then said, "I guess you could call me semi-lapsed."

"What does *semi-lapsed* mean?"

Marty chuckled. "It means no one tells me what to do, and I show up when and where I want. That's not how it's supposed to work in the Way."

"How is it supposed to work?"

"Are you guys taping this?" Marty asked.

"Do you have any objections to our taping?" Mr. Miller asked.

"Not really. But I don't want to get in trouble some way for talking about the trial."

"We won't be asking you about that," Mr. Miller assured him.

"I just wanted to know what was going on."

"Thank you. We really appreciate that."

"So how is it supposed to work – in the Way? It's called the *Way*? Am I right?" Ms. Blaze asked.

"Here's how it works. The head servant tells all the other servants what to do, and they tell all the lay people what to do and what not to do. You have to go to assembly on Thursday night and fellowship on Sunday and you have to let servants sleep in your house. You have to go to retreat twice a year. That about covers it. If you don't do that they get their undies all in a wad."

"What do these people think about Miss Kite?" Ms. Blaze asked. "Are they taking her side or the victim's side? Or are they being neutral?"

"They're probably all over the place. They really don't know how to be neutral, but this case is different because the *accused* and the *victim* are of about equal status – you know, both servants, both young ... cousins to boot. Everyone's probably more worried about themselves than they are about Amber and Orville."

"Do you know Amber and Orville personally?"

"Oh yeah, both of them, since I was small."

"What do you suppose happened?"

"Who knows?" Marty replied. "I guess we'll just have to wait and see what comes out in court."

"I've tried to get some information on this religion, but I can't find anything anywhere. If you research *The Way* on the Internet you come up with everything but this religion."

"I wrote a book about this group," Marty said. "It's a history of the Way."

"What's the name of the book?"

"It's called *The Way – from Ohio to Poppy Hill*. It gives the whole history on how it developed to its present organization. They have an interesting history, I should say."

"Where can we get this book?"

"It's readily available," Marty said. "In fact, I won a Pulitzer prize for it."

"Oh, my, my," Ms. Blaze said. "I have to check this out."

Marty chuckled.

"Do your pastors promote your book for you?"

"Never," Marty laughed loudly. "They wanted everyone to burn it. I'm a major embarrassment to them now, I guess."

Suddenly, as if on cue, the cameras stopped recording and the two gentlemen moved on. But Ms. Blaze was still interested. "Are you going to be here this afternoon?" she asked.

"Yeah."

"I'd like to talk to you some more about this group, if it's okay."

"Sure."

Hattie and Edith were met by B.J. as they emerged from the courthouse. Before they got far from the entrance three others caught up with them. They were the servant and the couple who had taken seats on the far side of the courtroom from them.

"Good morning, folks," Patrick, the servant, greeted them. "Are you folks going somewhere for lunch?"

"We're going to that little café down the street," Hattie said. "Do you care to join us?"

Oh no, Edith thought. *How can I possibly talk to these people?*

"Sure," Patrick said. "Do you know this couple, Edith?"

"Oh yes," Edith replied. "I know Rex and Bunny. How are you folks?"

"Just fine," Bunny said.

"And this is Edith's son, B.J." Hattie explained.

At the table, Patrick began with, "This is a difficult time for you, Edith."

"Yes, it is."

"For sure something good will come out of this," Hattie pointed out.

After a pause Patrick said, "You're probably right."

"Every cloud has a silver lining," Hattie purred on. "We have no idea what is going to be good for God's kingdom."

B.J. and Edith had no idea what to say. There they were in the company of two servants and two Way friends they hardly knew – none of whom they had enough confidence in to confide any of their true feelings. B.J. was uncomfortable with the situation.

"For sure the Lord will intervene and cause the right outcome," Patrick continued.

"For sure," Rex agreed.

"Uncle Mark apparently is going to testify next," Patrick said.

"He'll be able to set a lot of things straight," Bunny opined.

"For sure," Patrick agreed.

"Have you ever heard of so many servants being on trial at the same time?" Bunny asked.

"Never," Hattie said.

"Actually, the only one on trial here is Amber," B.J. corrected.

Everyone looked at him.

"But it's unusual that servants ever go to court," Patrick explained.

"Actually, they've been *summoned* to court," B.J. continued. "They've been summoned because they're witnesses to something."

Hattie looked worried. Patrick stopped talking. Bunny looked uncomfortable, and Rex studied his food. Edith patted B.J.'s knee to warn him to be quiet.

B.J. knew all too well why she did it. In the Way you needed to be wary of presenting any opinion one of the servants may not subscribe to.

"Well, did you see who was talking to the television people?" Patrick asked.

"No," Hattie said. "We were told not to talk to news people."

"It wasn't one of the servants," Patrick explained. "It was that kid Marty Spinner."

"Who's he?" Bunny asked.

"He's that guy who wrote that blasphemous book," Rex whispered to her.

"Oh!"

"This is all we need," Patrick sighed. "Someone like him blabbering away to the media. Uncle Mark should have gotten a restraining order against him."

"Why do they need to have anyone else testify anyway?" Bunny queried. "Don't they already know who did it?"

"You know lawyers," Patrick said. "They have to drag things out so people will forget why they went to court in the first place."

"Where are poor Orville's parents today?" Bunny asked. "Can you imagine how that poor young man felt coming in there today and being asked questions like that?"

"They're coming into town later today to take Orville home for a while," Patrick said.

"He'll definitely need a rest after this morning," Bunny sympathized.

"If we could only get Marty Spinner out of town," Patrick wished.

"I read his book," Hattie interjected.

The others all stared at her.

"It was very informative," Hattie added.

"I thought we were instructed to burn that book," Rex said.

"We were," Hattie smiled. "I read it before I burned it."

Patrick looked at her curiously.

"What was the book about?" Edith asked.

"No one needs to know," Patrick advised. "It could be damaging to your faith."

Poor Mom, B.J. thought. *They have nothing to say to comfort her today.*

"I'm going to be anxious to hear what Mark says in court this afternoon," Bunny said enthusiastically. "Will we be taking notes?"

"I don't know," Hattie said.

"Someone probably will," Patrick said. "I saw one of the friends there this morning, and she takes shorthand. So maybe we'll get a full copy of what he says."

"Wouldn't that be wonderful," Bunny said. "I've never heard of a head servant testifying in court. This will be just like Jesus being on trial. Wouldn't it be something wonderful for all our friends to read?"

There were a couple of quiet murmurs of agreement.

"He won't be able to give a sermon," B.J. reminded them.

Edith put her hand on this knee again, so he said nothing more.

"Well, we'll see," Patrick acknowledged.

While they were leaving the café Patrick said to B.J., "Surely your mother doesn't believe Amber will get off with this."

"Actually I'm encouraging her to hope she will," B.J. replied.

"Well, it would be nice for her if that were possible," Patrick allowed. But he sounded like he didn't believe it would happen.

"Out of curiosity, does Mark know you're here?" B.J. asked.

Patrick flushed, and glanced at Hattie, who was smiling wryly. "I'm on my way from Sacramento to Poppy Hill," he explained. "So I thought I'd stop by here for a while."

Ah, B.J. concluded. *He's cheating on Uncle Mark's orders!*

CHAPTER 9

PROSECUTOR: Mr. Volpe, can you tell us what your position is in the Way?

MARK: I'm the head servant, or head minister, for California.

PROSECUTOR: And as such, what are your responsibilities?

MARK: I oversee the work of the ministry, and manage its affairs.

PROSECUTOR: And this includes planning for your semi-annual retreats.

MARK: Yes, it does.

PROSECUTOR: Now at the time of this mishap in Poppy Hill, you were also the head servant at the time. Am I right?

MARK: That's right.

PROSECUTOR: Tell us what you witnessed in Poppy Hill the night Mr. Voigt was shot.

MARK: I was awakened by one of the servants and called out to help with the situation. First of all, I went and woke the owner of the property because he has a helicopter. I figured it would be the fastest way for us to get Orville to the hospital.

PROSECUTOR: Who is the owner of the property?

MARK: Victor Bergman.

PROSECUTOR: Continue.

MARK: Then I went to the dorm where the women were sleeping and I asked for one of them to come and help us. I knew she was a nurse, so I figured she would be the best person to help us.

PROSECUTOR: Tell us what her name is.

MARK: Lois Snyder.

PROSECUTOR: Continue.

MARK: So while they were tending to Oliver a couple of others were making a makeshift stretcher so we could put him in the helicopter. Then, when Mr. Bergman was ready, they took Orville to the helicopter and they left for the hospital in Bakersfield.

"I was there," Hattie whispered. "For some reason they never woke me up that night. It's kind of scary to find out you've slept through a shooting incident."

"I can imagine," Edith agreed.

"See that young man over there in the green shirt?" Hattie pointed to someone Edith didn't recognize.

"Yes."

"That's Marty Spinner. He's the one who wrote the book we were supposed to burn."

"He looks like a decent young man," Edith commented.

"Yes, he does, doesn't he?"

CLAY: Good afternoon, Mr. Volpe.

MARK: Good afternoon, Clay. (Mark smiled.)

CLAY: (Clay did not smile back.) Mr. Volpe, please tell the court under what circumstances you became head servant?

MARK: Uncle Floyd passed away, and he had designated me to be his successor.

CLAY: Now, *Uncle Floyd;* is that a title?

MARK: Yes. We call our head servants *Uncle*.

CLAY: And the legal name for Uncle Floyd would be?

MARK: Floyd Toner.

CLAY: What preparation did you have for this new stewardship?

MARK: I spent several years being tutored by Uncle Floyd in preparation for this new position.

CLAY: Now, in your opinion, have you effected any changes in the practice of your faith, or in the qualifications for your ministerial offices?

MARK: Absolutely nothing has changed. It's my duty as head servant to assure that none of our practices or customs change. We believe the Way is God's correct way, and that it must forever remain the same.

CLAY: Concerning the use of guns and other weapons – do you have a policy among your people about the possession and use of weapons?

MARK: We never tell people what to own in their homes. But we servants do not *believe* in carrying weapons, we do *not* carry weapons, and I have *never* known a servant who carried one; much less used one.

CLAY: Did you know that Miss Kite had a weapon in her possession?

MARK: No.

CLAY: Do you know where she may have acquired the weapon?

MARK: No.

CLAY: Who is in charge of security at your retreat facilities?

MARK: Uh, I guess I am.

CLAY: But is there someone who actually *acts* as a security person?

MARK: Someone will patrol the grounds at night to make sure no one comes onto the property.

CLAY: Was there someone patrolling the night of this incident?

MARK: I don't think so. The retreat had still not begun at that time.

CLAY: And when there is someone on patrol, what happens if someone happens to come onto the property?

MARK: They're instructed to call the police, or an ambulance, whichever is needed.

CHAPTER 10

CLAY: And if someone attending the retreat causes a problem?

MARK: I've never known of anyone attending a retreat who needed to be removed. We have the most peaceful and law abiding people in our group. Occasionally someone will become sick and need help, though, and the security person would be directed to call an ambulance in that case.

CLAY: Can you explain why there was no such person on duty on the night of this incident?

MARK: Like I said, retreat hadn't yet started.

CLAY: How many people were sleeping on the retreat property that night?

MARK: Probably seventy five people, in all.

CLAY: Now, who did you say it was who notified you of the shooting that night?

MARK: One of the servants.

CLAY: Which servant would that be?

MARK: Delbert Carpio.

CLAY: Did Delbert give you this news in person, or did he have someone else tell you?

MARK: Uh, yes, Lois Snyder came and told me what had happened.

CLAY: How long was it from the time you woke up until they actually put Mr. Voigt in the helicopter?

MARK: I don't know. It took a while – maybe fifteen minutes.

CLAY: I see. Now I have some more questions about your group.

MARK: Okay.

CLAY: You told the jury that this is a very moral and law abiding group of people.

MARK: Yes.

CLAY: How long have you been head servant of this group?

MARK: About a year and a half.

CLAY: And your predecessor, a year and a half ago, was Floyd Toner. Is that right?

MARK: Yes.

CLAY: And he was an upstanding character?

MARK: Oh yes.

CLAY: Did Floyd Toner have a clean record with the law?

MARK: Pardon me?

CLAY: Did Floyd Toner have a clean record with the law?

MARK: Uh, well, what do you mean?

CLAY: Was he ever convicted of a crime in a court of law?

MARK: Oh. Well, he had one error.

CLAY: What was that error?

MARK: He neglected to report a person for molesting some children.

CLAY: How long ago was that?

MARK: About three years ago.

CLAY: And who was it he neglected to report?

MARK: It was Howard Barnes.

CLAY: Why did Mr. Toner have a responsibility to report Mr. Barnes to the law?

MARK: Mr. Barnes used to be a servant.

CLAY: So Mr. Barnes was a minister who had been molesting children?

MARK: But he is no longer a servant.

CLAY: Was Mr. Barnes in the Way ministry when he was arrested?

MARK: Uh, yes, I think so.

CLAY: How long ago did that incident occur?

PROSECUTOR: Objection, your honor. This case is not about either Howard Barnes or Floyd Toner.

JUDGE: Mr. Shipman?

CLAY: No, this trial is not about Howard Barnes or Floyd Toner. But I intend to make the case that these retreats are unsafe environments where the reputation of the group comes before respect for the law.

PROSECUTOR: I object, your honor. This has nothing to do with Miss Kite's actions that night.

CLAY: (He snapped immediately at the prosecutor.) I told you I'd give you what you wanted.

JUDGE: Pardon me, Mr. Shipman.

PROSECUTOR: It's okay, your honor. I withdraw my objection.

The judge looked confused for a moment, then settled the objection.

JUDGE: Then I will overrule this objection. But Mr. Shipman, be sure you tie this in to the circumstances of this case. Also, I do not want you addressing the prosecutor during these proceedings.

CLAY: I intend not to, your honor. And I apologize. I'll abide by your admonition.

JUDGE: You may continue with your cross-examination.

Edith was horrified. She looked around the room to see how other people were responding, and most looked shocked. Hattie's eyes were closed as though in meditation.

CLAY: Is it your claim that your servants remain chaste while in the ministry?

MARK: Yes.

CLAY: Do you know of any incidents of those vows being broken at retreats?

MARK: No, I don't.

CLAY: Are you aware of any incidents of sexual violence occurring at retreats?

MARK: No.

CLAY: None at all?

MARK: Certainly no sexual violence.

CLAY: Are you aware of any other acts of violence occurring at retreats?

MARK: No. None at all.

CLAY: These people who are involved with security at retreat – have they ever reported any intruders onto the retreat property?

MARK: No, not really. Once they called the police about someone who was playing very loud music on the street nearby at midnight.

CLAY: Was that in Poppy Hill?

MARK: No. That was in Rancho Cucamonga, the old retreat location. We have no neighbors in Poppy Hill.

CLAY: How long has it been since the retreat was moved from Rancho Cucamonga?

MARK: Two and a half years.

CLAY: In the past five years – have these security people reported any *intruders* onto retreat properties?

MARK: No. Certainly not in the last five years.

CLAY: You call your female servants *handmaidens*, am I right?

MARK: Yes.

CLAY: What is the consequence should one of your handmaidens become pregnant?

Mark hesitated, and looked from the judge to the prosecutor.

MARK: Oh, well, we would, uh, tell them to get married, I'm sure.

CLAY: The handmaiden and the man involved?

MARK: Yes.

CLAY: No other possibilities?

MARK: No. That's the biblical resolution for that sin.

When Mark left, Clay just couldn't resist the urge to pick up the phone and call his wife. "Nancy, are you sitting down? You're not going to believe this. Last night, Amber Kite shot Orville Voigt. Orville is in critical condition in the Bakersfield hospital, and Amber is in jail."

"I can't believe this. This is really unbelievable," Nancy exclaimed. "How did you find out? Who told you? Why did Amber shoot him?"

"I don't know the particulars yet, but I was approached by two different people today about the matter. Marty Spinner on behalf of Amber, and Mark Volpe."

"Here we go again," Nancy predicted. "As hard as this is going to be, my lips again are tightly sealed. Trust me."

"Like a good attorney's wife!" he chuckled.

That evening there was a short clip on the evening news on television. Clay's ears perked up the instant he heard the words "Poppy Hill".

"Let's now go to Poppy Hill where our newsman Jock Miller interviewed a resident of the religious community where a shooting occurred the night before last. What have you learned, Jock?"

"Good evening," Jock began. "I'm here in Poppy Hill, standing at the end of the narrow road leading to the retreat grounds of a sect called the Way. We can see a large house on top of this hill behind me – that's part of the religious community located up there. I was asked not to go up there by the owner of the property, but I have with me one of the residents from the community and he has agreed to speak to me."

"Nancy," Clay yelled, "Bart Stanley's on TV."

"His name is Bart Stanley, a senior member of the clergy here. What can you tell us about what occurred up there the other night?"

"We had a young lady with us who shot one of our young preachers," Bart stated nervously.

"Who was this young lady? What was her role in the community?"

"She was a preacher too." Bart tossed his head to one side. "But we don't know what happened to her. We expect she just took a violent turn or something. Lost her mind, or something. But we're grateful no one was killed and she's been safely removed from us now."

"How unusual is it for something like this to happen in your community?"

"It never happens," Bart averred. "We are strictly against violence of any kind, and we do not believe in the possession of weapons among us. It was totally inappropriate and absolutely unnecessary for that woman to have a weapon up there. We are the most peaceful group of people you'll ever meet."

"It's good to know that no one was killed. Thank you for speaking to us."

"You're welcome," Bart replied, and trotted off up the road.

"We have learned that the young man who was shot was flown to a hospital in Bakersfield," Jock continued. "We have just learned that he is still in critical but stable condition in the intensive care unit of that hospital."

"Thank you for that report, Jock," the news anchor replied. "And now let's hear what the weather is going to be overnight and tomorrow."

"I can't believe it! Bart Stanley just appeared on TV," Nancy laughed loudly. "He'll be in trouble when Uncle Mark learns about it!"

"Unless Uncle Mark goes to Wal-Mart to watch the news he's probably not going to ever know Bart was on TV."

They both laughed.

CHAPTER 11

Mark Volpe looked relieved to be allowed to leave the courtroom. Through the day the courtroom seemed to fill up with Way friends, and a few people looked disappointed that he didn't acknowledge them as he exited through the aisle.

The prosecutor then called Linda Bell. She was one of the emergency room nurses on duty the night Orville was taken to her hospital. She was only on the stand a very short time, and Clay looked rather bored with most of her testimony. The most important question they asked of her was what Orville told her before he was anesthetized for surgery.

BELL: I asked him who would do such a thing to him.
CLAY: And what did he say?
BELL: He said it was Tina somebody. I couldn't get the last name.
CLAY: Did Mr. Voigt have ID on him?
BELL: No. Aside from his bathrobe, undershorts, and sandals, all he had was a box of condoms in his pocket.
CLAY: I have no further questions.

While Ms. Bell was leaving the courtroom, Clay began talking heatedly with his secretary, who busied herself with something on her computer while the next witness was called in.

Dr. Lowell came to the stand and explained the extent of Orville's injuries. One of the bullets had passed through Orville's left side, narrowly missing his lung. "This," he explained, "was the only reason Orville survived. If it had passed just one inch to the left it would have punctured his lung and he wouldn't have survived the transportation to

Bakersfield, given that it had taken them more than forty five minutes to get him to the emergency room."

Dr. Lowell explained that the second bullet had grazed his left arm, probably because the first bullet would have knocked him nearly out of its trajectory.

Before the trial recessed for the day, Clay announced that he was going to recall Orville to the stand. And the day's proceedings were finished.

Outside the courthouse, most of the Way friends huddled in groups before dispersing. Marty hung around until Clay and his secretary came out.

"How did it go?" Marty asked.

"How do you think, Marty?" Clay asked.

"I'm impatient. I want to see how you're going to get Amber off. Surely you can't make anyone believe Tina did it even though Orville thought she did."

"This is the problem with eye witnesses sometimes," Clay explained. "They don't always see what they think they see."

"I find that really intriguing. I want to see how you get around that."

"Are you coming back tomorrow? We have the police investigator on the stand."

"I'll be here," Marty promised. "I have to go home tonight and finish a paper that I have to pass in tomorrow. If I shove it under the professor's door tomorrow morning I can be back here in time."

"Good. If you want to be a lawyer, this is a good trial to watch. Not overly complicated, an easy one to follow. I think."

"That's cool. I talked to a reporter today, but I don't think I told them anything they really wanted to hear."

Clay chuckled.

"But why are you having Orville come back?"

"I didn't know about the condoms until this afternoon."

"Oh." Marty laughed roguishly. "I have to hear that. Oh my gosh! And what was that about the prosecutor's objection?"

"He wants to question Amber, so I made a deal."

While Hattie and Edith were waiting for B.J. to meet them, Hattie said, "Uncle Mark told me Tiffany has to go back to Poppy Hill. But I'm staying here in town, so I was wondering, can I treat you and B.J. to a quiet dinner somewhere? Are you staying in town tonight?"

"Yes, we're staying in town," Edith said. "But you don't have to pay for our dinner."

"Oh, I insist," Hattie said. "I don't want to be visiting anyone else tonight."

"You're so kind. You're always so kind to people."

"Thank you dear," Hattie smiled.

At dinner Hattie said, "You know, B.J., I remember when you and Amber were small. You were the best little kids."

"And look what happened to us," B.J. replied.

"Life didn't give you an easy hand, did it?" Hattie offered.

Edith wiped her eye.

B.J. studied his mother, then said, "But we had the world's best mother."

"I know," Hattie replied. "I remember I was with Lois Snyder one time in San José when you lived there. Little Amber came to us with a problem, and Lois wasn't terribly helpful. I was sorry for Amber, but Lois has a very domineering personality and she made me keep quiet. I didn't agree with her advice."

"What was Amber's problem?" Edith worried.

"Well, I hope you won't be annoyed with me," Hattie lowered her voice. "But Amber was worried that her father was going to hurt you, and her too. She said Bernie was angry most of the time and she was afraid of him. She didn't like to hear you crying when he was mad at you."

"Oh dear," Edith sighed.

"Amber had a legitimate concern," B.J. said. "Dad really abused Mom. Amber and I were sick to our stomachs with fear most of the time he was at home. I want to know – did Amber tell you that he actually hurt them?"

"Don't dig too deep now, B.J.," Edith admonished him.

"It's all right," Hattie said. "We have our brothers and sisters to help us carry our burdens. You can share these things because, you know, people who are abused *need* the help of others. Most of all, they need to know that others care for them. There are too many bullies in the world."

"The Lord wouldn't give us more than we could stand, I guess," Edith commented.

"Oh!" Hattie corrected. "I no longer allow abused people to say such a thing. I've seen too many bullies run to the older servants and kiss up – good old boys' club, you know. The good Lord didn't bless anyone with a bully."

Edith looked shocked. Hattie sounded almost blasphemous with such a comment.

"I'm curious," B.J. said. "What did Lois tell Amber?"

"Basically what she said was that Amber's problem was nothing more than a private little family secret – that she should keep it within the family. She said Amber was a traitor to her family by talking about their secrets with others. She talked very sweetly to her – you know how sweet Lois can sound – but I could see that Amber wasn't comforted at all by her little lecture. You can tell when a child is afraid." She paused for a minute. "Actually, unless children that age aren't exposed" to "that age are exposed to such abuse they aren't able to complain about it with any level of credibility." There was another pause. "Actually, adults are so consumed with their own secrets that they don't have any time for the children – sometimes."

"We had a mother who made the time for us," B.J. assured her.

"I know that," Hattie agreed. "That's why you were such good children."

Tears dotted Edith's cheeks, but she said not a word. Her mind was wandering to the first insult in her marriage.

It was the evening of their honeymoon. They had a room in a hotel near SFO – they were leaving for Hawaii in the morning for a week.

They had gone into the hotel room, set their suitcases aside; and Bernie went to the easy chair, slouched down so he could spread his legs wide, and cupped his hands over his crotch. "Okay, baby, time for the show."

"What show?"

"The strip show," Bernie said. "You can start now."

"I don't know what you mean."

"Strip for me," he demanded.

"You mean take all my clothes off?"

"Of course. What did you expect?"

"I thought maybe you'd kiss me first, or something."

"I kissed you at the wedding," he said. "I'm not in the mood again just yet. Strip for me and get me turned on."

"I don't know how to do that," Edith pleaded.

"Okay, I'll tell you. First you come over here and stand in front of me. Okay, now you grind your hips and show me your tits."

"Bernie!"

"Go ahead. Do it."

"Why?"

"Show me something to get me in the mood," he said, massaging his crotch.

"I want to change to my pajamas first."

"Go get your pajamas and let me see them."

Edith opened her suitcase and pulled out her flowery pajamas, pantie-like bottoms and modest tube-style top. She held them up for him.

"You bought that for your honeymoon?" Bernie asked indignantly.

"Yes."

"And you thought that was sexy?"

"I wasn't expecting to put on some kind of show or whatever. I just thought …"

"That's never going to put me in the mood," he said, standing up. "Why don't you go to the bathroom and change and we'll get some sleep. We have to get up early in the morning."

"Okay." She fled to the bathroom to change.

When she emerged from the bathroom Bernie was already in bed with his back to her. The blanket was down to his waist and he was naked from the waist up. She pulled the blanket down to get into bed, and noticed that he was naked from the waist down too.

He didn't turn over, so she got into bed, pulled the blanket up, and said, "Good night."

He didn't answer.

She was a long time falling off to sleep. She felt like crying, but she was too confused to cry. She wondered how she could have been so naive that she didn't know what would be expected of her on her wedding night. And she remembered Kumar – she could never imagine him behaving the way Bernie had behaved. She just wanted to be held and kissed like Kumar did. And she felt ashamed for even thinking about that.

In the morning she was awakened by Bernie's hands exploring in her panties. "I'm in the mood," he was whispering in her ear.

Edith opened her eyes, and it was still dark outside.

Before she could wake herself thoroughly Bernie had removed her panties and rolled her over and proceeded to have sex with her.

He was rough. It hurt. He made noises, and she was relieved when it was over – except that he proceeded to kiss her passionately – and she wasn't in the mood.

"You can get up now," Bernie said. "We have to get to the airport."

CHAPTER 11

Marty was the first person to show up at the courthouse the next morning. So he wandered back and forth in front of the building across the street to see who'd be that day's attendees. *This is amazing,* he thought. *All these servants and handmaidens being called into court. There can't be enough of them left in Poppy Hill to prepare for retreat.*

The timing of the trial, right before retreat, had been a problem for Mark Volpe, apparently. He had called the prosecutor prior to the trial and asked if it could be delayed three weeks so he could hold retreat in Poppy Hill. The prosecutor promptly told Mark he should get some of his *servants* to take his place for the day while he testified. Mark had subsequently gone to see Clay in his office to see if he would ask to have the dates changed, and Clay informed him that he wouldn't do that, for a number of reasons. "You'll only need to be there one day," Clay also reminded him.

Yet Mark showed up again that second morning in Bakersfield – in a car with Tina Malek. It wasn't long before Bart Stanley showed up, alone. He didn't go inside – he just sat on a park bench nearby. *Nosey old geezer!* Marty thought. *I wonder why he and Mark didn't come here in the same car.* Then the Way friends started to arrive. He saw five cars driving into the parking garage, and he decided it was time to go inside himself.

"Young man!" Bart stopped him at the courthouse steps. "What are you doing here?"

"I'm attending the trial," Marty replied.

"You shouldn't be here."

"Why not?"

"You're out of favor with the servants."

"So?"

"So you shouldn't be here."

"Should *you* be here?"

"I'm here out of concern for the health of God's kingdom," Bart said in his own defense.

"This isn't Poppy Hill," Marty explained. "This is a public place. Look at all these other people going into the courthouse and they don't know anything about the Way. Pretend I'm one of them."

"They're not going in to *our* trial," Bart corrected. "They don't matter."

"Well, are *you* going inside?" Marty asked.

"No."

"What are you doing here then?"

"I, uh ... "

"You should be in Poppy Hill preparing for retreat, don't you think?"

Bart stared at him for a minute, then turned and walked away.

Marty chose a seat in the middle of the courtroom and listened to the others around him. No one knew who he was because he'd grown up in northern California. It was fascinating.

"Someone told me that Amber took the gun from Tina," one of them remarked. "What on earth would Tina have a gun for? I don't understand this at all."

"Do you suppose someone stole the gun from Victor's house?" another asked. "I didn't know servants could have guns."

"Someone told me Orville was in the ladies' restroom. What was he doing there? He knows where the men's room is by now, surely."

"Some people sleepwalk, you know."

"Amber has to have expected a problem or she wouldn't have had a gun."

"You know, if that Spinner kid hadn't written a book, the law wouldn't be involved with this at all. He brought all of this on us."

"But they had to take him to the hospital. He was dying."

"Isn't Lois a nurse?"

"Yeah, she's a nurse."

"Nurses don't operate on people."

"Why did they tell us not to come here? Look at all our friends who showed up. What's going to happen to them?"

"The servants are here too. What can they do to us?"

"Why is Uncle Mark outside again? Is he checking to see who else is coming to the trial?"

"If he is, we're all in trouble." That elicited a few snickers.

"Where's Amber's brother? I saw him outside. Why isn't he in here?"

"He wouldn't be any help to her anyway. He's a real hood. The last time I saw him he looked like he was dying. He's probably a drug addict by now."

"I was told he confessed again recently."

"He doesn't go to assembly, I was told."

"Where does he live anyway?"

"He used to live in L.A. I think he still lives there."

"I don't think he's really one of us. Bart Stanley told us he's a pervert, or something."

"Those poor kids must have been just drug up. What a shame!"

"What's Bart doing outside? Why doesn't he come in here?"

"Uncle Mark told him not to come here."

"Look at Hattie – sitting over there with Edith. They're not related to Hattie, are they?"

"Of course not. You know Hattie. She has to be looking after someone."

"Such a sweet old soul, isn't she?"

"Is Lois going to testify?"

"I don't know. I think they've had enough people already to decide what happened."

"I think Uncle Mark should have been keeping better track of things out there."

"What was Lois doing that night anyway?"

"Maybe Uncle Mark wasn't feeling well and needed something."

"He doesn't need anything in the middle of the night. Uncle Floyd probably did, but there's nothing wrong with Uncle Mark."

"I don't think Lois should help him like that. People would think something's going on. You know what people are like – they always assume the worst."

"I agree. They should have one of the young servants looking after the head servant, then no one would suspect anything inappropriate."

"Well considering what happened a couple of years ago, I don't think that would be such a good idea. If a young man were going to see him at night people would think he was having a homosexual affair."

"Don't we have a eunuch they could assign to that job?" That comment elicited some more muffled snickers.

"Oh, Mary, you're a case!"

Then everyone settled down because the court officials began preparing for the day's proceedings.

B.J. arrived, parked his car, and went into the donut shop across the street. Bart followed him in.

"Good morning, Bart," *What are you looking for this morning?*

"Good morning, B.J."

"May I join you?" Bart asked.

"Sure," B.J. said. *Now that you're here I'll make my time profitable.*

"Thanks," Bart said. He didn't object when B.J. offered to pay for his donut and coffee.

They took a table by the window, and B.J. said, "I've been wanting to ask you something."

"What's that?"

"I'm still wondering what you came to our house for that day when my Dad beat me so badly during lunch."

"I was hoping you'd remember that little lesson," Bart replied.

B.J. held back his anger. "But why were you there that day?"

"I was there because your father called me to come and give your mother some counseling."

"My mother?"

"Yes. Your mother was acting up."

"I don't understand. What do you mean?"

"She was not participating satisfactorily in the marital act, and your father needed some help."

"Really?"

"Yes. Your mother's a wonderfully good woman, but she did have just a flaw or two. One of them apparently was her unwillingness to fulfill some of her wifely duties."

"Mom did everything. We had the servants visiting us all the time and she always cooked meals and prepared the house for assembly and fellowship. She *slaved* for my father – until he took off and left her and us."

"That was too bad. If your mother could have served him appropriately he may still be in his home up north and serving as the wonderful bishop that he was."

"What was wrong with my mother?" B.J. insisted.

"She wasn't pleasing him in the bedroom."

"They had two children."

"Well, in a marriage the man is entitled to more than that. It's true that the marital act is for procreation, but males are made to have a lust that, and once yielded to, cannot be contained. That's what marriage is for – so that men can satisfy their lust. Then, if there are children, they're not bastards."

B.J. watched him intently. *You old bastard! You're enjoying this.*

"This is something you'll understand when you become married. This is why we want our servants to be virgins. Once a man yields to his lust, he cannot contain himself. So this is why a man's wife has a duty to service him. It makes it so his lust won't send him to a lost eternity by becoming adulterous."

"So what did you tell my mother?" B.J. asked.

"She listened really well," Bart assured him. "I told her that your father needed to satisfy his lustful nature on a regular basis, and I asked her if once a week would be satisfactory to her. She accepted that suggestion. Your father would have preferred three or four times a week, but he settled for once a week. He was a wonderfully accommodating man."

"Why do you suppose their marriage didn't work in the end?"

"I expect your mother didn't keep her end of the bargain," Bart opined. "It's usually the woman's fault, because it's of no great consequence to her. Women don't appreciate that that's their role in a marriage, unfortunately. It's a common problem, I understand."

"For what it's worth, I believe my father raped my mother – frequently."

"She was his wife!" Bart seemed exasperated.

There was a pause, then B.J. asked, "So what do you think of my mother now?"

"A wonderful woman. Just a wonderful woman."

"She redeemed herself?"

"Yes, she did. I'll explain how. When the time came that your father left her, I advised her that it would not be appropriate for her to seek a divorce, so she didn't divorce him. And she didn't take up with another man. This is great evidence of her obedience to the Lord."

"Really?"

"Oh yes. And I'll tell you why. That godly woman, when her husband left her, also took my advice and refused to ask for welfare. She went out and got a job so she'd not be a burden on society. She's much to be commended for that spirit in her."

Bart stopped talking. B.J. was telling himself, *Be careful how you say this or he'll get up and walk away.*

"I should tell you the rest of the story," B.J. began.

"The rest of the story?"

"Yes. What happened after she took your last bit of advice."

"I'd be interested in hearing that," Bart said sarcastically.

"My mother got a job, working at Kentucky Fried Chicken, because she had no work experience and it was sixteen years since she'd been in school. She worked six days a week, but after she made the house payment and paid the utilities she had only two hundred dollars for the three of us to live on. So we moved to a tiny two bedroom apartment and let the mortgage company foreclose on our house. All our friends said they were too busy to help us move, so one of my high school friends borrowed his father's pickup and helped us move what we could keep into our new apartment. We let him sell what he could of what was left in the house to pay for helping us.

"And a week after we moved, my Mom brought her two-week paycheck home and all she got was forty dollars. You would never guess why she only got forty dollars."

"I'm sure you're going to tell me." Bart sniggered.

"Because they were taking child support payments out of her ... for some kid somewhere that my father had with another woman."

"They can't do that," Bart protested. "That's a lie."

"This is a community property state, Bart, and when they can't collect a bill from one person they can take it from that person's spouse. My mother was still married to my father."

Bart stared at him.

"So – she had eighty dollars a month for the three of us to live on. Do you suppose she could pay the rent with that?"

Bart was still staring at him.

"Hattie bought us dinner last night and the bill came to fifty dollars, for the three of us. Over half my mother's monthly income." There was a pregnant pause. "Anyway, my Mom still refused to go looking for welfare, so how do you suppose we lived?"

Bart shrugged, but didn't say anything.

"What do you suggest people do in such a situation?"

"The Lord provides for his own," Bart blurted.

"How do you suppose He provided for us?"

"I'm sure you have an ingenious answer for that."

"The Lord found *me* a job ... delivering drugs for the man who used to sell them to my *father*. Just by chance the man decided he was getting too much attention at an apartment building in Oakland, so he asked me to deliver for him three times a week. I got a hundred dollars every time I delivered. That's how we lived."

"So you were a drug dealer," Bart concluded.

"The Lord provided," B.J. reminded him. "We got quite hungry after that forty dollars was gone."

"Does your mother know what you were doing for money?"

"I never told her. But there was one good thing about it."

"What was that?"

"When I came home I didn't drop drugs into my mother's orange juice ... in an attempt to get her to try some wild sexual fantasy with me ... like my father used to do. He was a good bishop, wasn't he?"

"Shame on you," Bart barked.

"I beg your pardon?"

"I said shame on you for living off the profits of illegal drug trafficking."

"But it was you who told her not to divorce my father, and it was you who told her not to live off the tax money the rest of our Way friends were paying for the benefit of destitute single mothers like mine." B.J. stood up. "I appreciate all you've done for my mother and Amber and me. But we survived a lot more comfortably when there was no more starving in the house and I was able to pay for her divorce and she didn't have to pay child support for my father's bastard child we never met. You never once came back to see how well we lived on our twenty bucks a week, did you?"

B.J. left because he was about to cry. He went quickly to his car so he could weep where no one would bother him.

CHAPTER 12

Some people were satisfied, after the first day of the trial, that enough testimony had been presented to find Amber Kite guilty. But when uniformed officer Flores was called to the stand there was the expectation that he'd shed more light on the incident.

PROSECUTOR: When did you get to see the victim?

FLORES: I was on the helicopter pad when they landed at the hospital.

PROSECUTOR: And who was in the helicopter?

FLORES: There was the victim, Mr. Voigt; the helicopter pilot, Mr. Bergman; and a lady, Miss Snyder.

PROSECUTOR: Tell us what occurred at the hospital.

FLORES: Mr. Voigt was not really lucid at the time. I understand he told one of the nurses who it was who shot him, but I wasn't present when he did that. I spoke individually to Mr. Bergman and Miss Snyder, and neither person seemed to know exactly what happened. Both said they'd been told that a lady named Tina shot him, but they weren't clear on that.

PROSECUTOR: When were you able to speak to Mr. Voigt?

FLORES: I later spoke to him briefly in the intensive care unit at 320 hours and he said he thought it was the young lady named Tina who shot him. But he told me he wasn't sure of that.

By the time the sun was about to rise, Officers Flores and Clausen were at the retreat property in Poppy Hill. Poppy Hill is a tiny dilapidated village an hour out in the desert east of Bakersfield.

PROSECUTOR: Tell us what you found at the scene in Poppy Hill.

FLORES: Officer Clausen accompanied me to Poppy Hill, and we found a rather chaotic scene at the site. There were approximately one hundred people there and they were all concerned with tidying up after the shooting. I immediately told them to stop, and we secured the area they identified as the shooting scene and we began our investigation. Much of the evidence a the scene had been destroyed. The gun was missing, and the bullets were reported to have been thrown away. The blood on the walkway had been washed up.

PROSECUTOR: Tell us how you determined who exactly it was that fired the gun.

FLORES: Officer Clausen and I identified individuals who could help us fit together what happened, and we found that Miss Kite, of her own admission, had fired the gun and then dropped it. Miss Kite also said the gun was hers.

PROSECUTOR: And was the weapon recovered?

FLORES: Yes. The gun was found about forty feet away from the restroom in a grassy area, and it was found to have Tina Malek's fingerprints on it. According to both Miss Kite and Miss Malek, Miss Malek had picked up the gun and thrown it away into the field behind the ladies' restroom.

PROSECUTOR: Can you describe the weapon that was used?

FLORES: Yes. It was a featherweight Smith and Wesson, pearl handled, gold triggered, with a titanium cylinder.

PROSECUTOR: Do you recognize this as the weapon you recovered?

FLORES: Yes, that's the weapon. I've never seen one exactly like that before.

PROSECUTOR: Did you, in fact, connect this weapon to Miss Kite?

FLORES: We were able to recover two bullets from a trash can in the ladies' restroom. They were 110 grain Winchester silvertips, hollow point. We located an envelope in Miss Kite's suitcase that had three other bullets of the same type. Miss Kite's fingerprints were found on those bullets.

PROSECUTOR: Was Miss Kite lawfully in possession of this gun?

FLORES: No. The gun was not registered, and Miss Kite did not have a permit to carry a concealed weapon.

PROSECUTOR: Now we need to know how you determined malicious intent on the part of Miss Kite.

FLORES: Among items found in Miss Kite's suitcase was a journal, or a diary, in which we found Mr. Voigt's name and her wish that he would go home and never come back.

PROSECUTOR: Did she write *why* she didn't want Mr. Voigt to come back.

FLORES: No.

PROSECUTOR: Were there others in the book that Miss Kite wanted to be rid of?

FLORES: Yes.

PROSECUTOR: Who were they?

FLORES: Her father was the first person she apparently did not like. She wrote that she wished she didn't have to see him any more. She then wrote that she did not like someone called Lois. It wasn't clear what her problem was with Lois, but at one point she said she was glad to not have to deal with her any more. Then, at some later date in the journal, she began writing again about this Lois person, and she wrote that she'd put up with her as long as she could and if she couldn't take any more she'd have to do something radical to get away from her.

PROSECUTOR: Were there any others?

FLORES: There was someone she called Uncle Floyd. Several times she wrote that she was terrified of him, and wrote: *The next time this happens I'll deal with him the way he needs to be dealt with.* Shortly afterwards she wrote: *He's gone. God will forgive me – I no longer have to deal with him.*

There was a hushed din of whispering through the courtroom. The diary was entered into evidence, and the jurors appeared eager to peruse its contents.

PROSECUTOR: Were you able to find any indication for why Miss Kite was so angry with these people?

FLORES: No. That was unclear. But the journal is replete with angry writings and wishes to be relieved of these people's presence.

PROSECUTOR: Over what periods of time did Miss Kite write these entries in her diary?

FLORES: These writings are dated over a period of sixteen years, the last entry being just a year ago.

PROSECUTOR: Were you able to find any other items related to this incident in Miss Kite's possession?

FLORES: No. She apparently lived out of her suitcase.

PROSECUTOR: When was Miss Kite arrested?

FLORES: She was arrested that day during the investigation. We determined we had ample information to charge her with assault.

PROSECUTOR: So why are we now dealing with an attempted murder charge?

FLORES: It was the contents of the diary that prompted that change. We considered her writings evidence of motivation.

When the prosecutor had no further questions, Clay announced that he wouldn't cross examine the officer. Immediately the prosecutor announced that the prosecution would rest. There was a flurry of paper moving and whispering around the tables at the front of the courtroom, and everyone waited to see what would happen next. After a short recess called by the judge, the proceedings resumed.

CLAY: The defense calls Tina Malek to the stand.

The courtroom was hushed as Tina took her place on the stand. She was the epitome of a modest, sober, and composed young lady. She wore a midi-length dark green pattern dress, and had her long hair exquisitely swirled into a tidy bun on the back of her head.

CLAY: Can you tell the court what you know about the events of that night in Poppy Hill?

TINA: I was asleep in the handmaidens' dorm ... well, I was awake, in bed. And I heard a popping noise, twice, outside the door and then the door opened and someone was screaming. So I got up to see what was happening, and it was Amber. She was hysterical.

CLAY: Did she say anything?

TINA: She said she shot someone ... a man, who was coming into the yard between our dorm and the ladies' restroom.

CLAY: Did she say who it was?

TINA: No. She said she didn't know who it was.

CLAY: What did you do then?

TINA: I went to the gate and looked out, but there wasn't anyone there, so I tried to calm her down.

CLAY: What happened after that?

TINA: Well, Lois came in, Lois Snyder, and asked us what happened, and I told her that someone got shot, and she tried to help me calm Amber. She wanted us to go outside so we wouldn't wake up the other handmaidens, but Amber was afraid to go outside. By that time a lot of the other handmaidens were awake anyway and asking what was going on. Lois told them, "Go back to sleep – we'll find out in the morning." But then there was a huge knock on the gate, and Amber screamed again, and I think everyone woke up.

CLAY: Who was at the gate?

TINA: It was Uncle Mark – Mark Volpe. He wanted Lois to go and help someone outside. Some of us followed her outside and tried to see what was happening over by the men's dorm, but we couldn't see much. The lights were on inside over there, and we saw them pick someone up and head for the helicopter, and Lois went with them. And Uncle Mark came back and told us all to go to bed.

CLAY: Did you all go to bed?

TINA: A couple of us. No one went to sleep. Amber couldn't sleep, and I was scared.

CLAY: Why were you scared? Was it because the intruder had not been identified, or found?

TINA: No. I was scared because ... well, I knew who it was.

CLAY: You knew who was shot?

TINA: Yes.

CLAY: Who did you think it was?

TINA: Orville Voigt.

CLAY: How did you know that?

TINA: He was coming to see me that night.

CLAY: Were you expecting him?

TINA: Yes.

CLAY: Why were you expecting him?

TINA: He told me he was coming to see me after midnight.

CLAY: Can you tell the court why he was meeting you?

TINA: He wanted me to go with him to the pond.

CLAY: What happens at the pond?
TINA: Uhh ... sometimes people swim there.
CLAY: At midnight?
TINA: Yes.
CLAY: Who swims there at night?
TINA: Only servants, I think. I was never there when anyone else was swimming – just when Orville was swimming.
CLAY: So you would go out there to swim and then go back to bed?
TINA: Well, no.
CLAY: What else, then?
TINA: Well, I wouldn't go swimming in the dark.
CLAY: So *you* didn't go there to swim.
TINA: No.
CLAY: What did you go there for?
TINA: Orville told me to go there.
CLAY: What, in fact, did *you* do when you got there?
TINA: Do I have to say it here?
CLAY: Yes. Remember, you are under oath.
Tina lowered her head and breathed deeply.
TINA: Orville went there to have sex.
CLAY: With you?
TINA: (Long pause) Yes.
CLAY: Frequently?
TINA: About two or three times a week.
CLAY: Did anyone else know about this?
TINA: I don't know. No. One time we went out there we met Norman coming back.
CLAY: Norman who?
TINA: Norman Coombs.
CLAY: What was he doing out there that night?
TINA: I believe he was watching out for the property. He was always saying he liked to be out at night ... when it was quiet.
CLAY: And he was okay with you and Orville being out there at night?
TINA: Yes. He didn't say anything.
CLAY: And there was never anyone else at the pond while you were there.

TINA: Right.

CLAY: Did you ever go to the pond at night alone?

TINA: Never.

CLAY: These dates that you had with Orville – were they consensual?

TINA: What do you mean?

CLAY: Did you agree of your own free will to meet him there?

PROSECUTOR: I object, Your Honor. What difference does this make to this case whether Miss Malek consented or not?

CLAY: (He glared at the prosecutor.) I intend to show that the dangerous environment at this retreat involved not just potential harm to individuals, but coercion as well. It has already been established that Miss Kite expressed fear of a number of people who were on that property that night.

JUDGE: Overruled. And Mr. Shipman, please look at me when you are addressing *me*.

CLAY: My apologies, Your Honor. Miss Malek, did you agree of your own free will to meet Mr. Voigt at the pond?

TINA: Well, kind of.

CLAY: What do you mean by *kind of*?

TINA: He wanted me to go there the first time for just a walk, and I thought that was all he wanted.

CLAY: Who proposed that you have sex?

TINA: He did.

CLAY: Did you say *yes* or *no*?

TINA: I said I didn't think we should do that.

CLAY: What was your reason for not wanting to?

TINA: We weren't supposed to be doing that. I didn't want to get pregnant. I was afraid we'd get caught.

CLAY: So why did you not just refuse?

TINA: I was too afraid to run away alone in the woods in the dark. (She paused.) He told me he had protection.

CLAY: So you had sex with him.

TINA: Yes.

CLAY: Did Amber Kite have any knowledge of these meetings? Would she have expected to meet Orville there after midnight?

TINA: I'm sure she didn't.

CLAY: Did Amber have anything against Orville that would make her want to hurt him?

TINA: No. Amber thought the world of him. Orville's her cousin.

CLAY: Did Orville have anything against Amber?

TINA: No.

CLAY: Did you feel safe going out at night on the retreat property?

TINA: Not if I had someone with me.

CLAY: What would you be afraid of if you were alone?

TINA: It's dark out there at night. There are no street lights. And anyone could come into the retreat property and no one would know anything about it.

CLAY: Had anyone else ever been afraid to go to the restroom at night?

TINA: Always.

CLAY: Why were they afraid?

TINA: We'd always heard of things happening at night at retreat. That's why Norman patrols the property at night.

CLAY: What kind of things were rumored to happen at night?

TINA: There were rumors of kids misbehaving and doing damage. If we had to use the restroom in the night we'd just run to the ladies' room and then run back – if it was after dark.

PROSECUTOR: Miss Malek, you weren't clear on whether or not you wanted to have sex with Mr. Voigt. Did you or did you not want to have sex with him?

TINA: I did not, really.

PROSECUTOR: Then he did force you?

TINA: (She shrugged.) I don't know.

PROSECUTOR: You must know whether he forced you or not.

TINA: He just came to me and did what he wanted.

PROSECUTOR: Did he prevent you from running away?

TINA: No.

PROSECUTOR: So why did you continue to meet him?

TINA: He said if I didn't come out he'd bang on the wall of my dorm.

PROSECUTOR: And why didn't you want him banging on the wall? No one would know he was looking for you.

TINA: I was afraid he'd say he was looking for me, and I was afraid he'd say I'd agreed to meet him. And then they'd ask questions and maybe find out what we'd done, and I'd get sent home from the service. I was afraid that would happen.

PROSECUTOR: Did you ever tell him in the daylight that you didn't want to go there any more?

TINA: Yes.

PROSECUTOR: And what was his response?

TINA: He said, "You'll like it. I'll see you at twelve."

Needless to say, the whole courtroom was abuzz when the court recessed for lunch. Marty was trying to read the faces of all the Way friends in the room, but there was no show of emotion – except for a few looks of complete bewilderment.

In front of the courthouse they were in animated conversation.

"Why was he asking her those questions?"

"That was disgusting."

"Sickens me."

"What has become of Shipman since he stopped going to assembly?"

"I tell you, it's Satan. He's just driven to publicly shame God's servants. Evil."

"I'm not coming back here."

"I wouldn't blame you. I don't think I'll come back either."

Marty met B.J. on the sidewalk. "How you doin', buddy?"

"Good," B.J. said. "So what happened in there this morning?"

"Oh! The shit really hit the fan! You gotta hear this stuff."

"Not now, you realize."

"I realize. I'll tell you later."

"Sure."

CHAPTER 13

CLAY: Do you know where Miss Kite's handgun came from?
B.J.: Yes. I gave it to her.
CLAY: Why did you give her the handgun?
B.J.: I felt she needed it. She didn't want to take it, but I insisted she take it and use it if necessary.
CLAY: Please explain to this jury why you would insist on her taking this handgun.
B.J.: She took a leave from the service for a year and a half, and when she told me she was going to return to the service I insisted she take the gun with her for protection.
CLAY: For protection from whom?
B.J.: From other servants.
CLAY: You felt she needed protection from other servants?
B.J.: Yes.
CLAY: Why would you feel she needed protection from other servants?
B.J.: While she lived with me we talked a lot about what it was like to be in the service. And I wasn't happy with her decision to return. Everyone was told she had a problem with her nerves, but she and I were really taking care of each other. I was deathly ill at the time and she was trying to recover from an assault she'd been subjected to at retreat.
CLAY: Are you talking about physical assault, or verbal assault?
B.J.: A serious physical assault.
CLAY: What kind of physical assault?
B.J.: Sexual assault.

CLAY: And because of this you felt she needed a weapon to keep herself safe?
B.J.: Yes. Absolutely.
CLAY: Have you ever been to one of these retreats?
B.J.: Yes. I've been to a lot of them.
CLAY: Have you ever been assaulted at one of these retreats?
B.J.: No.
CLAY: Have you ever witnessed someone being assaulted there?
B.J.: No.
PROSECUTOR: Mr. Kite, you're a member of this religious group, are you not?
B.J.: No.
PROSECUTOR: You're not?
B.J.: I am not.
PROSECUTOR: Is it not true that you formally rejoined this group about one year ago?
B.J.: Yes, that's true.
PROSECUTOR: Have you renounced your membership since then?
B.J.: No, not formally. I just quit.
PROSECUTOR: Did you quit because of more evidence of violence?
B.J.: No. I quit because they wouldn't allow me to be baptized.
PROSECUTOR: Because they wouldn't let you be baptized?
B.J.: Right. They wouldn't allow me to confess, so I went to Ensenada and confessed down there.
PROSECUTOR: You confessed to what?
B.J.: That's what it's called when you join the Way. And when I came back to California they wouldn't recognize my confession, so I quit.
PROSECUTOR: I'm curious. Why would they not let you ... confess in California?
B.J.: I have AIDS.
PROSECUTOR: Does having AIDS exclude you from being a member of this faith?
B.J.: No. But the servants thought I was a danger to the rest of the people. I never intended to tell them I have AIDS. I never told

people I have AIDS. But they wanted me to confess to exactly how I'd contracted the disease, and I ... I wasn't about to discuss that.

PROSECUTOR: Then how would they know you have AIDS?

B.J.: One of the nurses in the clinic where my doctor works is a member of the Way, and she told the servants. It was illegal for her to tell them, but by then the servants knew and that was the end for me.

The prosecutor looked confused. Apparently that line of questioning wasn't serving his purpose, so he moved on.

PROSECUTOR: Now this gun that you gave to your sister – where did you get it?

B.J.: It was given to me.

PROSECUTOR: By whom?

B.J.: A lady I know.

PROSECUTOR: Do you know the lady's name?

B.J.: Yes.

PROSECUTOR: What was her name?

B.J.: Theresa.

PROSECUTOR: Theresa who?

B.J.: I don't know her last name.

PROSECUTOR: So you were given a gun by a lady whose last name you don't know.

B.J.: I don't know her last name. She called herself Theresa.

PROSECUTOR: Why did a woman whose last name you don't know give you a gun?

B.J.: She owed me some money and couldn't pay me, so I accepted the handgun as payment.

PROSECUTOR: What did she owe you for?

B.J.: For taking her to Las Vegas.

PROSECUTOR: For taking her to Las Vegas?

B.J.: Yes.

PROSECUTOR: Why did you take her there if she couldn't pay you?

B.J.: Well, she paid me ahead of time. But she borrowed some of it back so she could gamble and lost too much of it at the tables. And she couldn't pay me in full.

PROSECUTOR: Women pay you to take them places?

B.J.: Sometimes.

PROSECUTOR: Can you explain that?

B.J.: It's a lucrative line of work.

The prosecutor was again becoming confused. Marty, being his smart and smutty comedic self, was grinning from ear to ear.

PROSECUTOR: Let me ask you about these servants in this group. Can you tell us why exactly you believe your sister needed protection?

B.J.: I feel some of the servants are prone to violence.

PROSECUTOR: But you've told this court that you never witnessed any violence yourself.

B.J.: That's true. But I know one of the servants punched a kid in the face one time at retreat. I just didn't see it.

PROSECUTOR: Then that's hearsay.

B.J.: I know. But I saw the kid's nose bleeding. And I did witness some violence in my own house.

PROSECUTOR: By a servant?

B.J.: Yes.

PROSECUTOR: Tell us about that.

B.J.: A servant by the name of Bart Stanley came to my house after I'd asked to renew my membership – to check me out, probably. When he saw I had a radio sitting on my kitchen cupboard he unplugged it and threw it in the trash can. He doesn't believe in radios. And he pulled some posters off my wall and tore them up. They were posters of famous movies, and he doesn't believe in movies.

A couple of times the prosecutor asked B.J. to tell him what happened to Amber at retreat, but Clay persisted in objecting because it would be hearsay. Edith was a wreck when B.J. finished. She was trembling, so Hattie put her arm around her and comforted her. She was further comforted when B.J. skirted around the back of the courtroom and slipped into the seat beside her.

Hattie relinquished her hug so B.J. could put his arm around Edith. "I didn't know you were that sick. Why didn't you tell me?"

"I knew you'd worry," B.J. said. "But I'm fine now."

CHAPTER 14

CLAY: The defense calls Douglas Ferguson.

Douglas was one of the Way friends in his fifties, and lived in Arizona.

CLAY: Have you ever been to one of these retreats in California?

DOUGLAS: Yes, we came to one three years ago. It was the last one held in Rancho Cucamonga.

CLAY: Why was it that you came to retreat in California?

DOUGLAS: Our daughter lives in Escondido and we were visiting her. So we went to retreat with her.

CLAY: What kind of experience did you have at that retreat?

DOUGLAS: The retreat was fine. But my car was vandalized. We found that the radio antenna had been broken off overnight.

CLAY: Did you happen to park your car overnight at the retreat?

DOUGLAS: Yes, we did.

CLAY: Did you report that to the police?

DOUGLAS: No.

CLAY: Why not?

DOUGLAS: The servant I talked to told me they didn't want the police involved because they weren't sure it was an intruder from the street.

CLAY: Did he have a suspect?

DOUGLAS: No. I was told that just in case it turned out to be one of the kids at the retreat who had done it, it would be better if the police weren't involved. So I just had my car fixed when I went home.

CLAY: Were any other cars damaged at that time?

DOUGLAS: I saw two others.

CLAY: How were they damaged?

DOUGLAS: They both had their radio antennas broken off.

CLAY: And no one had any idea who would have done that?

DOUGLAS: There was one lady I spoke to who told me she'd seen one of the servants doing it when she was out to the restroom that night.

PROSECUTION: Objection, Your Honor. Hearsay.

JUDGE: Sustained.

PROSECUTOR: Would the insurance company not repair the damage to your car?

DOUGLAS: No. Because I hadn't filed a police report.

PROSECUTOR: Why would people at the retreat suspect it could be kids from the retreat who did this vandalism?

DOUGLAS: The servants in California don't believe in having radios, so I guess they didn't want antennas on cars. Kids sometimes take things too far.

PROSECUTOR: Surely there were more than three cars at the retreat with radio antennas on them.

DOUGLAS: Yes, there were. But the only three with broken antennas had Arizona plates. That's all I know.

PROSECUTOR: And you did not file a police report.

DOUGLAS: No. The servants told me not to.

PROSECUTOR: But you could have had your car repaired.

DOUGLAS: I don't disobey the servants.

Then Clay called Myrna Joyce.

CLAY: Ms. Joyce, you claim your son was assaulted at a retreat two years ago.

MYRNA: Yes. That's true.

CLAY: How old is your son?

MYRNA: He's ten now, but he was only eight at the time.

CLAY: Tell us what you know of the circumstances of this assault.

MYRNA: Well, my husband doesn't belong to the Way, so I used to take Mike with me to retreat. I had pushed my luck by taking him to sleep with me in the women's dorm until he was seven, so I decided he should go and sleep with some of the boys in the men's dorm. And that's where he was punched in the face – by one of the servants.

CLAY: Do you know the name of the servant?

MYRNA: Yes. It was Norman Coombs.

CLAY: Did Norman admit to punching Mike?

MYRNA: Yes. He said he only slapped him, but all the other kids near Mike said Norman had punched him.

CLAY: Did Mr. Coombs tell you why he'd done such a thing?

MYRNA: Yes, he did. He said that all the kids were acting up in the dorm and he wanted their fathers to straighten them out. But Mike's father wasn't there, so he had to do something as a surrogate father.

CLAY: Did Mike admit to acting up?

MYRNA: Oh yes. He told me they were all throwing peanut shells at the old men on the other side of the shed. He said he was doing it because all the other boys were getting away with it.

CLAY: How did you feel about Mr. Coombs hitting your child?

MYRNA: I was furious. Mike ran across the yard to me in the women's dorm with a bleeding nose. His nose was broken, and I had to take him to the hospital.

PROSECUTOR: Why did you send your son to sleep in another dorm with no one to supervise him?

MYRNA: I didn't. The father of his little friend said he'd watch out for Mike for me.

PROSECUTOR: So why did this Mr. Coombs undertake to discipline him?

MYRNA: I don't know. I suppose he thought it was his business, he being a servant and all and my son's father not being there.

PROSECUTOR: Who took Mike to the hospital?

MYRNA: I did – in my own car.

PROSECUTOR: Did you file a police report?

MYRNA: No.

PROSECUTOR: Why did you not file a police report?

MYRNA: I was told not to, but I knew better than to file one anyway.

PROSECUTOR: Who told you not to?

MYRNA: The head servant – Mark Volpe.

PROSECUTOR: Tell me, why did you know not to file a police report anyway?

MYRNA: There's a teaching in the Way that you do *not* take your brother to the law. I wasn't inclined to argue about that at that hour of the night.

PROSECUTOR: Did they not ask you in the hospital what happened to him?

MYRNA: Yes, of course, they did.

PROSECUTOR: What did you say?

MYRNA: I said he fell and smashed his nose on a cement floor.

PROSECUTOR: You lied.

Myrna just stared at him.

PROSECUTOR: I said you lied.

Myrna burst into tears.

PROSECUTOR: Why should we believe anything else you tell us?

MYRNA: Because I only lie ....

PROSECUTOR: About what?

MYRNA: Well, only if it's going to hurt the Way.

PROSECUTOR: But it was only Mr. Coombs who struck your child, not the whole Way population.

MYRNA: But he's a servant.

Then Clay called Trent Hansen to testify. Trent had been a servant for two and a half years, and then mysteriously ran away one day before retreat with another young servant who was reported to have been gay. The Way friends were quite confused about why Trent would run away with such a person. The truth was that it was Trent who was gay, not the other servant.

CLAY: Are you familiar with what went on at night during retreat?

TRENT: Yes. Quite familiar.

CLAY: Did you participate in any kind of mischief yourself?

TRENT: All the time.

CLAY: Did you ever get caught?

TRENT: We normally didn't get caught because we never made any noise. But one time we almost got caught.

CLAY: Tell us about that.

TRENT: One of my buddies had a pickup truck, and he brought it to retreat. He used to sleep in the back of it sometimes. One night he told us we should all go to his truck and have a beer, so we all went out there to the back of the orchard and sat around in the back of his truck and started drinking beer.

CLAY: Who provided the beer?

TRENT: My friend did, the driver of the truck.

CLAY: Were any of you old enough to drink legally?

TRENT: No. We were all in our teens.

CLAY: So what happened?

TRENT: We started talking about what we'd do if we each had a girl there and soon one of them pulled it out and started ... you know.

CLAY: Started what?

TRENT: Masturbating.

CLAY: And then what happened?

TRENT: Then a couple of others did the same. I think we were getting a bit drunk. We ended up all seven of us were doing it.

CLAY: So then what occurred?

TRENT: Norman Coombs came by and sneaked up on us and the first thing we knew he was looking over the side of the truck, watching us.

CLAY: Who is Norman Coombs?

TRENT: He's the servant who always wanted to go out at night and watch.

CLAY: As in *night watchman?*

TRENT: Well, yeah, but *we* always thought he just liked to *watch*.

CLAY: Watch?

TRENT: Yeah. He always hid and watched. He never reported anyone. No one ever knew he was watching them.

CLAY: Did you get in trouble for your underage drinking?

TRENT: No. All that happened was that none of us felt like ... you know ... finishing what we were doing.

PROSECUTOR: You mean this group tolerates underage drinking?

TRENT: No. But they're not going to report anyone for it either.

PROSECUTOR: I thought this group didn't believe in drinking, period.

TRENT: They don't, except for wine when they have services.

PROSECUTOR: So why were you not disciplined.

TRENT: Because Norman liked to watch. If he'd told on us he wouldn't get to watch things at night any more.

PROSECUTOR: Would any other night watchman have told on you?

TRENT: Probably.

PROSECUTOR: What would happen then?

TRENT: It would all depend on who you were. Some people would get kicked out of the Way, and others would just beg and plead for forgiveness and then be allowed to stay around ... I guess.

PROSECUTOR: And no one would have reported anything to the police?

TRENT: Oh no. They don't do that.

"Mercy, mercy!" Hattie sputtered. "If I'd known *that* was all happening while I was sleeping out there I'd have been sick to my stomach."

B.J. chuckled. "It's good you were getting a good night's sleep through it all, Hattie."

"I should say so."

"What else are we going to hear about before this is all over?" Edith worried.

"We'll just wait it out, dear," Hattie said. "We can get through this, you'll see."

Outside, Marty caught up with B.J. and said, "Man, I'm so sorry. I had no idea you had AIDS."

"I'm okay."

"I shouldn't ask, but how ..."

"I'll tell you. When I was a kid, delivering drugs to Oakland. One night I didn't have as much as the guy had ordered, so he and his friends fucked me up the ass before they let me go home."

"Holy cow! I don't know what to say."

"I'm okay. We'll talk sometime."

CHAPTER 15

STEVE: My name is Steve Gentry.
CLAY: Mr. Gentry. Were you a servant in the Way at one time?
STEVE: Yes.
CLAY: When was that?
STEVE: For about six months, beginning just before Christmas. Not last Christmas, the one before that.
CLAY: Can you describe your first week in the ministry for the jury?
STEVE: Yes. I arrived ten days before the retreat started and I was helping them prepare for the retreat. But on the second day there I got really sick. I had cold sweats and terrible pains in my stomach. And then I began to vomit. I had salmonella poisoning from something I'd eaten.
CLAY: Were you the only person who got salmonella poisoning?
STEVE: No. There were about eighty or ninety people there and I think everyone got sick. Not everyone got as sick as I did.
CLAY: How sick did you get?
STEVE: When I began vomiting and having diarrhea they told me to go and stay in a small tourist trailer someone had left at the retreat, and I stayed there for the rest of my time there.
CLAY: By the rest of your time, how long do you mean?
STEVE: I was there for four days before the retreat started and I was there for all of the first day of retreat.
CLAY: What kind of care did you receive?
STEVE: At first they brought me something to eat, but I couldn't eat it. I only threw it up. And I had to run to the restroom every half hour.

CLAY: Did you ask to see a doctor?

STEVE: Yes, I did. But they didn't want me to see a doctor. They gave me something someone brought from Canada, called *extract of wild strawberry*. It was supposed to work wonderfully, but I just got sicker and sicker.

CLAY: Why didn't they want you to see a doctor?

STEVE: They told me that if I went to a doctor, the doctor would report my case to the health department and they'd probably shut down the retreat.

CLAY: So how did you recover from your illness?

STEVE: My family came to retreat and when they couldn't find me anywhere after the first day my mother asked one of the servants where I was. The servant told her I was in the tourist trailer because I wasn't feeling well. When my Mom found me she was very upset. I was so weak my father decided to help me into his car and take me to the hospital. I was put on intravenous for a few days until I started to recover, and then I had to go home and rest for a week before I could go and join my companion.

PROSECUTOR: Why did you not just take yourself to the hospital?

STEVE: I couldn't. I had no vehicle and there was no vehicle available to me.

PROSECUTOR: Could you not have called a taxi for yourself?

STEVE: I had no money. I gave them all my money when I arrived at the retreat.

PROSECUTOR: You gave them all your money?

STEVE: Yes.

PROSECUTOR: Is that normal?

STEVE: If you want to be a servant, yes. You aren't allowed to own any property.

PROSECUTOR: You make it sound like they didn't take adequate care of you.

STEVE: They didn't. I needed intravenous and they wouldn't allow me to access it.

PROSECUTOR: So you were the only one who went to the hospital. Am I right?

STEVE: No. There were three others who never recovered on their own.

PROSECUTOR: They went to see a doctor?

STEVE: Yes.

PROSECUTOR: And was the retreat closed down?

STEVE: No. They kept the health officials away until the retreat was over.

PROSECUTOR: Was this really a life threatening event.

STEVE: I think you can die from salmonella poisoning. Vomiting blood and having bloody diarrhea aren't exactly healthy things.

During a break, the prosecutor turned to Clay and said, "Can I ask you a question?"

"Sure."

"Where did you find all these people?"

Clay smiled. "You must have missed them. There are a lot more where they came from."

"Sounds like a goddam cult to me."

"Could be."

Marty caught up with Clay. "Hey. Isn't this a crazy trial?"

"How do you mean?"

"Well, I can't understand why the prosecutor's asking a lot of the questions he's asking. Isn't he just helping you make your case?"

"That's the point," Clay agreed.

"How come he's doing that?"

"It's easy. I call all the people I want *him* to question. I get to ask them questions first, and then he doesn't know what to do with them."

Marty looked surprised. "Wow! What a trick!

"A strategy I don't always share, okay."

"Cool," Marty said, open-mouthed with admiration. "You're making him curious enough to ask for the worst details, and I think it makes him look like he doesn't really know what kind of people he's talking about. Right?"

"Here's some advice for you. Take philosophy courses on critical thinking and reason. You'll understand why they're important courses for a trial attorney. This guy needs a refresher course."

"I'll look for those courses. Thanks."

"Are we going to be able to go home tomorrow night?" Edith asked as they were eating dinner.

"Maybe so," B.J. said. "Clay thinks he can finish up tomorrow."

"That'll be good," Hattie said. "This is very tiring, isn't it?"

"Very tiring," Edith agreed. "And I can't understand why you never told me before. I didn't know you were that sick, B.J."

"You'd worry about me, wouldn't you?" B.J. smiled. "My doctor convinced me I'd get better, so I didn't think you needed to know how sick I was."

"But you still haven't told me that Amber was assaulted. I didn't know that until you told them in court."

"I know," B.J. said slowly. "You'll hear more about that tomorrow, maybe. But don't worry, she'll be okay."

"You think so?" Edith asked.

"Sure. Amber and I look after each other."

"Isn't that wonderful," Hattie interjected.

"Hattie, do you believe that Amber was assaulted at retreat?" Edith asked.

"My dear," Hattie began. "I'm old enough to believe anything. Yes, I expect she was if she says so. It's terrible!"

They were quiet for a long time.

"It's hard to believe," Edith said sadly. "For the first eighteen years of my life I thought it was absolutely impossible for someone in the Way to do anything wrong or hurt anyone else. I guess that's not true."

"Unfortunately, it happens," Hattie sighed.

B.J.'s mind wandered to the day he told Amber about his diagnosis. He'd written to her and told her he was very ill and didn't want Edith to know about it, and mentioned that he was going to need someone to stay with him in case he needed some help. She had shown up at his apartment door a week later and announced that she was going to stay with him.

"But you're a handmaiden," B.J. protested. "Why did you leave to look after me?"

"Right now I'm not a handmaiden," Amber said. "I had to leave for a while."

"Why?"

"Not now. I came to look after you. You look like you're dying. What's wrong with you?"

"I have AIDS."

"What?"

"I have AIDS."

"How?"

"I don't know. Really, I don't know for sure."

"Were you shooting up, or were you ... you know."

"No," B.J. said. "I have never used drugs. Never."

Amber was quiet for a while.

"Here," B.J. said. "Put your things in this closet." He took a couple of jackets out of the closet and threw them on a chair.

He made Amber some coffee, and they sat at the table.

"Do you know what I was doing when I was sixteen?" B.J. began.

"Mom told me not to ask you."

"I was delivering drugs – for the man that Dad used to buy his drugs from."

Amber was shocked.

"I got over a grand a month for it," he said.

"You're lucky you didn't get caught."

"I almost did a few times. But I was really careful."

"You don't do that now, do you?"

"Oh no. I found another way to make money."

"Dare I ask?" Amber inquired.

He hesitated. "While I was in Oakland one night this guy offered me fifty dollars to ... I shouldn't tell you this, but he said, *Ain't you the cutest thing that ever walked. I'd blow you for a price*. So I told him I'd need fifty dollars and ... that was it."

"B.J.! You didn't!"

"That's not all," he continued. "The next time I got a hundred dollars."

"B.J.!?"

"You know, if you go really high class you can entertain for parties. It's a lot better than hanging out with drug dealers. That's where I'd go when I didn't come home until morning."

"You dropped out of school," Amber protested.

"But we lived."

"What did they pay you for at parties?"

"Well, I'd dress up, or dress *down*, and serve drinks, or anything that was going."

"Why would they pay you to do that?"

"I was young, big for my age, I had started to work out, and some people thought I was good looking, and I was ... well, they thought I was, you know, *big*. Rich guys pay for anything. You don't really need to do much – just be there."

"I don't know what to say." Amber shook her head. "I didn't know you were gay."

"I'm not."

"Oh."

"You just close your eyes and think of money."

Amber was horrified.

"When I came to L.A. I worked almost every night in clubs – dancing. The money was really good."

"So this dancing – are you telling me that you were stripping?"

"Yeah."

"Oh my goodness, B.J.!"

"I had no education, and the money was good. So I went to a school and got a G.E.D. and then went to college. That's how I got through college."

"I didn't know that."

"Yes. I earned it all myself."

"Are you still doing ... you know?

"No. Look at me. I'm a scarecrow."

"Is that how you got AIDS?"

"I don't think so. I'm sure it wasn't." He paused, then said, "I was gang raped in Oakland."

They were quiet for a long while. Then B.J. asked, "Where is Harvey Koontz these days?"

"He's around. He was at retreat just recently. Why do you ask?"

"I saw him a while ago."

"Where?"

"I was dancing in a gay club and he wanted a date, so I went with him to a hotel room down the street. He paid me three hundred dollars."

"B.J., stop this. You're lying."

"Oh no, I'm not lying." Then he laughed.

"What's so funny?"

"After he was done I asked him if he knew who I was, and he said *no*. So I told him I was B.J. from San José and he says, *Oh shit!* He told me he'd been kicked out of the service because *he* was gay."

"He was never kicked out of the service," Amber corrected. "He's still a servant."

"No kidding," B.J. chuckled. "He was good, though. Best blow job I ever had."

It was an abrupt catching up he and Amber had that day. He was relieved to see her, and she was glad to be there.

"Well, you sure don't look as healthy as you did a couple of years ago," Amber said. "If your doctor says you can get better, I'll help you until you are."

"Thanks for coming," he said. "I need some help. I'm too weak to do anything for more than an hour or two, and then I'm totally exhausted."

"And let's just not tell Mom what's wrong with us, okay?"

"No." Then he broke out in tears. "I'm so sorry?"

"What for?"

"Everything. I just feel like lying down and never getting up. Look at me. I've just ruined my life."

"No," Amber said. "You fed Mom and I for years and you have a college education. Don't ever say that about yourself again. You have years ahead of you."

"But if Dad hadn't been ... "

"It's okay, B.J. We can do it without him."

"I wanted to get married and have a family."

And they held each other and wept.

CHAPTER 16

The servants and handmaidens sat around the table in Poppy Hill that evening and made small talk, all patiently waiting to hear news from the trial in Bakersfield. They were one week away from retreat, and the last minute preparations were their prime concern – unless the trial got mentioned. No one really knew what to say about the trial. First they'd been forbidden to discuss it, then once the topic came up that was all they wanted to talk about. But only in small settings, for fear of offending the sensitivities of someone who may be of an opposing opinion about the whole matter.

When the meal was over, Mark Volpe opened up his laptop and read an e-mail from one of the Way friends who'd sat in on the trial all that day. Everyone listened in silence as the lengthy e-mail was read.

"So there you have the latest," Mark said when he finished.

"Uncle Mark," one of the older handmaidens spoke up. "Will this e-mail be shared with all the Way friends in California?"

Norman Coombs got up and left the dining hall.

Lois Snyder followed him.

Bart Stanley was all ears.

"I don't think it would be advisable," Mark replied. "This would likely be harmful to the faith of some of our friends, and it wouldn't be wise to expose them to such ... nonsense. I'm going to ask that anyone who has this e-mail not to pass it on."

There was a long pause. Sober faces lined the tables.

"It would be best if we ignore this," Bart spoke up. "These things may not be true at all."

"It would just be better if they were not discussed," Mark corrected. "Strong meat is only appropriate for those who have matured enough to have their senses exercised to discern good and evil."

"Yes," someone murmured. "That's scriptural, isn't it?"

"Of course," Mark agreed.

Everyone got up and fulfilled their responsibilities in cleaning up after dinner.

It was not until a couple of hours later in their dorm that a number of handmaidens got into a discussion about the trial.

"I think I'm confused about this," Sandra said. "What's the difference between *good* and *evil*?"

"The difference between *good* and *evil* is this," Charlotte explained. "*Good* is in accordance with the will of God, and *evil* is what is *not* in accordance with the will of God."

"So what's going on with this trial?" Sandra persisted. "Someone damages people's property at retreat – is that good or evil?"

"That's evil," Monica said.

"Well, not necessarily so," Charlotte corrected. "People should not be showing the world that they listen to the radio. So they don't need radio antennas."

"Does anyone except the Way friends care whether you have a radio or not?" Monica wondered.

"The point is, Monica, people only notice things that are different – they stand out to people." Charlotte was adamant. "People will notice when a car has no radio antenna, and they'll ask why our friends don't have one."

"Do you really think so, Charlotte?" Sandra asked.

"Of course, dear. The same with Christmas decorations. When people see a house that doesn't have Christmas decorations, they know there is something very special about those people. Only dead fish go with the flow, you remember."

"Well, I guess Muslims are alive after all," Tanya tittered.

"But Muslims do *strange* things," Charlotte agreed. "They don't respect established Christian beliefs, and they hide in their wraps. That's not a good example of anything to the world. They're just looking for attention with all that stuff. Our Way friends only do things that God established to make them stand out in the world. Righteous things.

You see, we just stand out. Not to get anyone's attention – just because we reflect what God has made of us."

On the other side of the dorm some other handmaidens were listening, and having their own whispered conversation.

"Personally, I'm not interested in being assaulted, here or anywhere else," Brenda announced. "I think that's just evil, period."

"I know," Laura agreed. "I get really upset when they start rationalizing such things. I've never been assaulted by anyone, but I know what I'd do if I were. I was a tomboy growing up. I could do something about it."

"I don't know if that would help," Brenda warned. "I think if you fight back they would find a way to send you home."

"Don't they care what we think of them?"

"What we think of who? Uncle Mark and the older servants?"

"Yeah," Laura said. "Don't they care how we feel?"

"Listen to what Charlotte's telling them now," Brenda said, nodding her head in Charlotte's direction.

"You see, girls, when the men are speaking, they're speaking for God," Charlotte explained. "But when women speak up, they're denying their very nature. We're to be in submission to the men because that's the position God has called them to."

"She believes that, doesn't she?" Laura whispered.

"What do you think of that attitude?"

"I used to hate it, really. And frankly, I thought a few times I'd lose my mind over that. But then after a while something came over me and I just don't think of it any more."

"That's because no one's assaulted you yet," Laura speculated.

"Well, not physically, at least."

"You mean you've been assaulted some other way?"

"We all have," Brenda assured them. "Every time you get called down they tell you something to make you feel low and mean – *disobedient* is the word. It's to make us feel humble."

"I thought it was only me who got that."

"Everyone gets it. They just don't dare let on they've been insulted beyond belief."

"Once when I was a companion to Wilda she told me I looked like a tramp," Laura confided.

"How would she know what a tramp looks like?" Brenda shrugged. "I suppose it was because you let your hair fall over your ear or something."

"No. I have some hair that used to pop out of my bun and fall down on my face, and she told me it made me look like a tramp. So I got some scissors to trim it and she threw a fit. I had to start putting my bun on the top of my head so that piece wouldn't slip out and people wouldn't see it."

Brenda shrugged. "Yup! And listen to this." She nodded again in Charlotte's direction.

"I'm not so sure we should have a lot of sympathy for Amber's brother," Charlotte was telling the others.

"Why not?" Sandra asked. "Someone told me he was a really nice guy."

"Oh no," Charlotte corrected. "I was told by Harvey Koontz that he's known to be a prostitute?"

"A prostitute?"

"Yes," Charlotte said. "Can you imagine? I know Bart praises Edith to the highest, but I don't know. I think Edith could have brought those two kids up better than she did. Imagine – a handmaiden with a gun! And at retreat, no less! Have you ever heard of such a thing in your life?"

"What was Orville doing at the ladies' room after midnight anyway?" Monica asked.

"My dear, don't even think about that," Charlotte advised. "You'll think of nothing good, when all along he may have had a perfectly legitimate reason for being there. We'll never know why he was there until he tells us some time."

"Charlotte," Sandra protested. "Tina said herself that Orville was coming over here to meet her."

"I don't believe that," Charlotte said. "I'm sure Clay persuaded her to say that in court just to help get Amber off. That doesn't change the facts at all. And to think that man was once one of us. I desperately fear for that man's soul."

In the men's dorm things were quiet that evening.

"Where's Norman?" Ned asked.

"I saw him going for a walk," Lloyd replied. "Out toward the pond."

"He's probably gone out to see if anyone's skinny dipping," Gordon snickered.

"Did you say skinny dipping?" Troy asked. Troy was a novice servant that year.

"Yeah," Ned said. "There's a rumor going around that someone goes skinny dipping in the pond."

"Really?" Troy was aghast. "That's where they have baptisms."

A couple of them laughed, and one of them quipped, "Skinny dipping doesn't necessarily pollute the pond, they've discovered."

"Norman probably wouldn't even bother checking, except that there'd be a chance he'd see someone naked," Ned laughed.

"Ned," Patrick said sternly. "That's enough."

"Sorry," Ned said contritely.

Ned winked at Troy, and Troy grinned timidly. Troy had only been there for two weeks, and he was on full alert for any clues about the correct way to behave among other servants. Ned had been reading the uncertainties in Troy's expressions those two weeks, and he'd given him hints about what he could and couldn't do.

"What are we going to tell the guest servants when they come in for retreat?"

"Don't worry. Uncle Mark will give them the official version."

CHAPTER 17

CLAY: The defense calls Connie Riggs Ho.

Everyone in the courtroom turned and watched with curiosity as Connie approach the stand. It was understandable, considering the apparent mess she'd made of her life. She'd been a well-liked handmaiden for hardly two years when she suddenly left the service and married a young servant named Vince Ho. It wasn't like such a thing hadn't happened before – it was just that it was always a shock when it happened. Aside from that, it meant the loss of two servants at one time, and the Way friends lamented any loss of servants.

Everyone was greatly shocked again when she left Vince five months later and absolutely refused to go back to him. The servants pleaded with her to do the right thing, but she was adamant in her refusal. She was pregnant at the time, and they tried to stress upon her the need for her child to have a father, especially if it were a boy. But she still refused.

The real shock came a month and a half later when she delivered a baby boy. And the baby was only a month premature – according to rumors.

CLAY: Please state your name for the record.
CONNIE: Constance Riggs
CLAY: Pardon me.
CONNIE: Constance Riggs. No, I'm not Connie Ho. I'm divorced and I have resumed using my maiden name.
CLAY: While you were in the service, did there come a time when you were assaulted?
CONNIE: Yes.

CLAY: By whom?

CONNIE: Vince Ho.

CLAY: Tell the court who Vince Ho was at that time.

CONNIE: He was a fellow servant, in the Way.

CLAY: Tell the jury the circumstances of your assault.

CONNIE: We were preparing for retreat at Poppy Hill, and he kept teasing me about playing with me. We were both young – I thought he was joking. So I would ask him, 'Where's your sandbox?' And he'd just say, 'I'll find one.' And every once in a while he'd say, 'I never got to play with a girl when I was a kid.' I really didn't take him seriously. Until one night I went out to the restroom after it was dark, and when I was headed back to the dorm he called me to the gate. So I went to see what he wanted. Just as I got there he grabbed my arm and said, 'Come with me. I found a great sandbox to play in.' I tried to pull away from him, but he was holding on tight and pulling me along. He took me behind the men's dorm where there was a storage shed, and he forced me down onto an old mattress that was there on the floor and … he raped me."

She began to weep. The bailiff gave her a box of tissues, and she regained her composure.

CLAY: So what followed then?

CONNIE: I, uh, had to go back to the women's dorm. But I couldn't sleep. I was scared and hurting. I had to go to the chiropractor two weeks later to have my jaw realigned because he'd held his hand over my mouth while he … did it. I found out later that I was pregnant, so I had to speak to Uncle Mark about it, and he told me I could either marry Vince or have an abortion. I decided I just could *not* have an abortion, so Uncle Mark talked to Vince and told him he had to marry me. So we were married.

CLAY: Did you want to marry Mr. Ho?

CONNIE: No. He'd raped me. And I wasn't in love with him. At that point I didn't even like him, but I didn't believe in abortion and I wasn't going to kill my baby, so I decided to live with it.

CLAY: How did that decision work out?

CONNIE: It didn't. (She paused.) He assaulted me several times, and my doctor reported him to the police and I left him. Then I divorced him.

B.J. looked around the courtroom, and the expressions on people's faces were amazing. Every expression of shock and dismay was showing. Hattie sat with her hands folded and her eyes lowered. Edith was sitting with her mouth wide open.

But they hadn't heard the worst part yet. The prosecution had to attempt to discredit her testimony – if he could.

PROSECUTION: Why did your superior not give you the option of having the baby without marrying the father, whom you say you didn't even like?

CONNIE: I could have, but if I did that I could be excommunicated.

PROSECUTION: Does your faith believe in abortion?

CONNIE: They don't. I was ... offended to be advised to have an abortion.

PROSECUTION: Why did your superior recommend abortion then?

CONNIE: He said it would save the ministry the embarrassment of having to deal with a pregnant handmaiden. Being unmarried and pregnant would mean being excommunicated.

PROSECUTION: So it was just about saving the ministry from embarrassment?

CONNIE: I think so. And he insisted he couldn't permit me to suffer the shame of having an illegitimate child.

PROSECUTION: But you divorced Mr. Ho. You didn't carry through with your conviction, did you?

CONNIE: I divorced him because he was beating me up about once a week and I was afraid I'd lose my baby.

PROSECUTION: Did you not report him to the police?

CONNIE: I wasn't going to, because we don't believe in reporting each other to the police. But after at least a dozen times (she sobbed.) my doctor reported him to the police and he was arrested. I was so relieved to have him away from me that I packed my things and went to live with my parents.

There was a lengthy pause.

PROSECUTION: Did you not report this rape to anyone when it happened?

CONNIE: No.

PROSECUTION: Why not?

CONNIE: There was no one to tell. We weren't supposed to call the police on each other.

PROSECUTION: Did you not go to the hospital or a doctor to be checked out?

CONNIE: No. They would have reported it to the police.

PROSECUTION: Did you not have any injuries?

CONNIE: Yes, I did.

PROSECUTION: Why did it take you two weeks to see a chiropractor?

CONNIE: I had no way to see one. I was needed for preparations for the retreat. And servants just never leave retreat without a good reason. Anyway, I was embarrassed, and I was probably an hour away from any medical help anyway.

PROSECUTION: How willing were you to go with Mr. Ho to his *sandbox*?

CONNIE: I wasn't willing at all.

PROSECUTION: Did you not call for help? Weren't there people within hearing distance?

CONNIE: I couldn't. He was holding his hand over my mouth.

PROSECUTION: Was there no one around who could have helped you?

CONNIE: There were maybe a hundred people around, but they were all asleep.

PROSECUTION: This court has already been told that there was a night watchman at these retreats.

CONNIE: There was.

PROSECUTION: And?

CONNIE: I'm not sure whether he happened to find us or if we just caught him watching.

PROSECUTION: But he didn't do anything to help you?

CONNIE: Obviously not. (She sounded exasperated.) A month later the head servant still didn't know anything happened.

Connie left the courtroom with her arms folded across her chest, her eyes on the floor, and glanced at no one.

"Are you okay, dear?" Hattie asked Edith.

Edith sighed. "Yes. I'll be okay."

Hattie patted her hand. "I have no idea why they needed to expose all of that."

The next person called to the stand was Robert O'Leary.
CLAY: Did you attend a winter retreat in California three years ago?
ROBERT: Yes.
CLAY: Which one?
ROBERT: It was in Rancho Cucamonga.
CLAY: Did you happen to have any unfortunate experience at that retreat?
ROBERT: Yes.
CLAY: Tell us about that.
ROBERT: My son was sexually assaulted in the men's dorm.
CLAY: What was the name and age of your son at the time?
ROBERT: His name is Andy. He was eight at the time.
CLAY: Tell me what occurred.
ROBERT: We were sleeping in the men's dorm, and my son was sleeping right beside me. And I discovered that the man on the other side of my son was molesting him. He was trying to take my son's pajamas off under his blanket.
CLAY: How did he have access to your son's blanket?
ROBERT: We were in bunks, side by side, with each person's head to the wall. The only way out of the bunk was from the foot of the cot. And all the man had to do was reach his hand over and touch my son.
CLAY: What brought this molestation to your attention?
ROBERT: I think there was a rustling in the cot beside me that kind of woke me up, and then I felt some movement in my son's cot. So I looked over and the man on the other side of Andy's cot was lying with his face up to Andy's and he was reaching under Andy's blanket. It was dark. I could hardly see what was happening.
CLAY: Go on.
ROBERT: I said to him, 'What are you doing?' And the man immediately pulled his hand back and turned over with his back to us. And Andy said out loud, 'Daddy, my pajamas are off.' I picked up his blanket and there were his pajamas down by his feet. I helped him

put them back on, and then had him trade cots with me so the man wouldn't bother him any more.

CLAY: Go on.

ROBERT: Andy didn't want to sleep alone on my cot, so I squeezed back onto my cot with him for the rest of the night.

CLAY: Did Andy tell you what the man was doing?

ROBERT: He just said he was a bad man and he was scared of him.

CLAY: Do you know who this man was?

ROBERT: Yes. He was Leroy Slepski. He used to be a servant. Everyone thought he was great.

CLAY: What did you do about this?

ROBERT: I told the head servant the next morning and all he said was that it was good I was there to look after my son.

CLAY: Did the head servant say anything about Mr. Slepski?

The prosecutor was becoming very agitated.

ROBERT: No. All he said was that I had to keep track of my son.

CLAY: Did you report this to the police?

ROBERT: No.

CLAY: Why not?

ROBERT: The head servant told me not to.

CLAY: Do you still sleep in the dorms at retreat?

ROBERT: No. Since that incident, we get a motel room and travel whatever distance it is each day to retreat.

The prosecutor declined to cross-question Mr. O'Leary.

CHAPTER 18

CLAY: Explain to the jury why it was that you first went into the service.

AMBER: I believed I was going to help people find God. I thought it was the highest calling for a person like me.

CLAY: You say for a person like me. What significance do you attach to that statement?

AMBER: I didn't want to get married. I'd seen my father beat my mother and abuse her, and I just couldn't allow myself to take the risk. And I was told that the only two possibilities for people in the Way were to either get married or go in the service.

CLAY: Were you happy in the ministry?

AMBER: Mostly, yes, I guess. I had a difficult time sleeping in a different bed every night. I found it hard to get used to having a different companion every six or twelve months or so. They all had different personalities.

CLAY: Was there ever a companion that you were particularly unhappy to be with?

AMBER: Yes.

CLAY: Who would that be?

AMBER: Lois Snyder.

CLAY: Tell us about Lois.

AMBER: I was assigned to be her companion four times. I always thought she disapproved of me. Her method of teaching me how to be a better handmaiden was to ridicule what I said or did, and then order me to do something different that she would explain to me. I'd be really depressed about that because I didn't need to be yelled at to do what I was told.

CLAY: Did this behavior on her part ever change?

AMBER: Yes. One day she came to me and praised me unbelievably, telling me that I was the best young handmaiden she'd ever been entrusted with.

CLAY: Did she say why she felt that way?

AMBER: She said that she'd never needed to tell me how to fix my hair, that all my dresses were always long enough, and I always did exactly what she told me. And I never did anything without her permission. She thanked me for not ever arguing with her when she ... corrected me.

CLAY: So things improved after that?

AMBER: No. It got worse.

It was at Rancho Cucamonga four years earlier, just before retreat. The morning after Lois had been so complimentary, she came to Amber again and wanted to talk some more. According to Lois, Mark Volpe had a medical problem that no one else knew anything about, but she had been assisting Mark with his treatment. She said she'd decided that she was going to need someone else to help her with the treatment, and she'd decided that Amber would be the best handmaiden to help her with that chore.

Everyone knew that Lois had been a nurse, and that she was very attentively taking care of Uncle Floyd at the time. Floyd was in his nineties and fragile, so Lois would frequently be seen going to his private cabin in the orchard. Retreat in Rancho Cucamonga used to be held in an orchard, and that's where Uncle Floyd would be resting. Sometimes she was seen taking him his dinner on a tray, and other times she was seen taking him his clean laundry. Most days he was able to come out of his cabin to observe the progress of the retreat preparations, but some days he just needed to rest all day.

Amber was flattered by the invitation, so she readily agreed to help Lois. After all, Mark had emerged as the heir apparent to Uncle Floyd's position. And among the handmaidens it was a very high honor to be selected for personal assistance to the head servant, and in this case the heir apparent.

Amber was also relieved that she wasn't asked to help with Uncle Floyd. She was scared to death of him. He was an austere man, stand offish, and the one who would expel someone from the service, without providing a reason. She had long dreaded what would become of her if he were to send her home. As long as she wasn't getting called into his presence she felt safe from being sent home.

That evening about seven thirty Lois told Amber they were going to pay Mark a visit in his cabin, in the orchard, near Uncle Floyd's cabin. It was a small, modest, but comfortable place. Aside from the bed, there was a dresser, a writing desk with a chair, and a comfortable recliner. Mark was sitting on the bed. Lois took the recliner, and Amber took the office chair. Amber thought there was going to be a discussion about the medical treatment that was required, but that was never mentioned.

"Lois gives me very good reports about you," Mark began.

"Thank you," Amber replied.

"You'll be a wonderful help to our work in California."

"Oh, thank you."

"I hope you have no doubts about continuing in the service."

"Oh no, none at all." Amber assured him.

"That's good. We need all the faithful servants and handmaidens we can get."

"I was sure before I came to the service that I was making this a life commitment." Amber had never considered leaving the service for any reason.

"A lot of people come to the service and have in mind the option of leaving if they don't find the lifestyle to their liking. But what we need is young people who are committed unconditionally for their lifetime. Sometimes there come very difficult tasks for servants and handmaidens, and we desperately need people with the strength to rise to the need. True servants never defect."

"I always try to do my best."

"Lois has assured me of that."

"Certainly," Lois confirmed.

"Thank you, Lois."

That was the content of the visit. As they were walking back to the handmaidens' dorm, Lois explained to Amber. "We'll probably have to help him tomorrow."

"This is a privilege," Amber said.

"Yes, it certainly is," Lois agreed.

It wasn't until the following evening at ten o'clock, lights out time at retreat, that Lois came to Amber and said they'd be going over to help Mark.

While Amber was testifying in court, Mark Volpe was in Poppy Hill in a private meeting with Percy Law, the head servant from Colorado. Percy was one of the guest servants for the retreat, and Mark had invited him to come early so they could take care of some business.

Not unexpectedly, the trial was on the agenda. Percy wanted to know how the trial was going, and Mark assured him that Amber would undoubtedly be found guilty. The facts were quite obvious – Orville had not attacked her, she had shot him anyway, and her possession of the gun was illegal to begin with.

Mark was concerned about what to do with Amber. He obviously didn't want her back in the service, but Floyd had never dealt with a shooting. So Mark had never been advised on how to deal with such a thing.

"Do nothing," Percy advised. "She should know she shouldn't come back, so just leave her off the assignment list for the next season. She should have been left off for the last year while she was waiting to be tried. She'll probably be in prison anyway."

What to do with Orville was another problem. He had been at home with his parents in Bishop much of the last year, and was listed as resting on the last servants' assignment list. He was by then feeling quite well enough to come back to active service, but Mark was concerned that his presence in the state would be a reminder to people of the shooting – and Mark wanted people to forget about that as quickly as possible. Also, he suspected the Way friends in California knew too much about the circumstances of the shooting to consider him qualified to preach the gospel.

Percy had actually come to California expecting to arrange an exchange of servants between the two states. He offered Mark a young servant named Alex, "... perhaps in exchange for Orville." Alex had never been out of Colorado, and Percy thought it would be good for him to have some exposure to the servants and Way friends in other states. Percy also expressed concern that Alex needed a strong tutor on Way doctrine, and Mark assured him that he could be a companion to Bart because Bart loved nothing more than to expound on doctrine.

The next matter Mark wanted to discuss was Norman. "Norman isn't doing all that well with the night watch, which he's insisted on doing for years now. I keep getting hints that he's not behaving well."

"What's his problem?"

"From what I can tell he's letting things happen that should never be going on at retreats. When I ask him about things I hear, he maintains that he never sees anything. This worries me. I've hesitated to forbid him to do night watch, but I think he's getting too familiar with some of our more wayward friends in the state."

Percy didn't say anything, obviously not being interested in having Norman move to Colorado.

"I'd like to see Tina Malek go to another state," Mark continued. "She's had some involvement in this shooting case, and it's not going to be good for the Way to have her in the state now, for the foreseeable future."

"But she's quite young, isn't she?"

"She is," Mark agreed.

"I need a strong, more senior handmaiden in Colorado because some of the younger handmaidens are getting a little too slack with their style of dress. Janet, my most senior handmaiden, has been in Colorado for a very long time, and she's a great example for them, but she won't confront them when they try such things as flowery buttons on their dresses. And I don't like these new colored rims on some of their eyeglasses. I'd really like to have someone like Lois in Colorado to help them with that."

"I can't let Lois go." Mark sounded surprisingly adamant. "Would you be able to exchange someone with Tina?"

Percy hesitated. "Where is Tina, anyway?"

Mark was put on the spot. She hadn't come directly back to retreat since she'd testified in court. There'd been whispering about that among the younger servants and handmaidens, and Percy had heard some of it.

"I've heard a disturbing rumor that she's had some inappropriate contact with a young servant," Mark admitted.

Percy withered at the comment, and he had some advice for Mark. He told Mark that if that were the case, Tina needed to be asked to step aside from the service – to protect the reputation of the ministry. "There seems to have been a rash of inappropriateness among the young servants here in California," Percy remarked. "You're going to have to get a handle on this, make an example of someone, or maybe a few, so it can stop. This is very damaging to the image of the ministry."

"Time to clean house, I guess," Mark thought out loud.

Mark explained that he'd never yet asked someone to leave the service, and he was dreading the need to do it. Percy volunteered to sit with him for the occasion, and he reminded Mark that any servant should always have another servant with him whenever he confronts anyone about a misdeed. "You know how rumors start. That's why the scriptures tell us to have at least two witnesses to a matter."

But Percy did get a concession from Mark with respect to Lois. Mark was going to allow Lois to go to Colorado as a guest speaker at their retreat in two weeks time, and Lois was to take a handmaiden of her choosing with her for the visit. "I may have a word with Lois about my concerns with the handmaidens in Colorado," Percy suggested, and Mark agreed it would be a good idea. Lois had skill at working timely admonishments into her sermons.

Another matter that Mark and Percy tackled was the proposal that the dishes used at retreats be replaced with disposable plates and cups. The head servant in Texas had made that change at retreats and claimed it made for a much faster cleanup after each meal – and in the end was not too expensive. Mark shared that he didn't like eating off paper plates, but Percy said that the servants' table would continue to use traditional tableware. Paper plates would be used on all the other tables. In the end Percy agreed to make the change in Colorado and let Mark know how it worked for him in Colorado.

During the past year there'd been a number of families that had moved each way between California and Colorado. Mark and Percy shared with each other matters of concern about these families, and

Percy had one caution. He said that the husband of one couple should not ever be allowed to become a bishop. The husband, Kurt, had operated a furniture business, and abruptly liquidated the business and moved his family to California. In the process, Kurt had failed to return to one of the Way friends in Colorado a large down payment she had made to him for some furniture. Mark decided he'd ask the servant assigned to Kurt's area in California to investigate how the man was conducting his business there.

Percy had another concern. "What do you know about Leon Jones?"

"Leon Jones – from Stockton. No one's mentioned anything about him. Do you know something I don't know?"

"One of the Way friends in Colorado has told me that Leon has been sharing with some of our friends back there that he's having Bible studies with a man who was put out of his assembly. I was wondering if you knew anything about that."

"I've not been made aware of that," Mark said. "There's a man who was expelled from his assembly in Stockton. I'll have to make a note to visit with Leon about that."

"You may have to ask him to stop participating in assembly," Percy warned. "We had a man in Colorado a couple of years ago who was doing that, and the first thing we knew he had a couple of other people wanting to have Bible studies with the expelled man too. It was a really dangerous affair. We can't have people taking control of their fellowship away from the ministry."

Before the visit was over, Percy had given Mark a standing invitation to the annual conference of the head servants in the Great Plains states. Mark always wondered why Floyd hadn't gone to any of those conferences, but Floyd never was one to go seeking advice from anyone. Mark was glad to accept Percy's invitation because his new role as head servant was at times overwhelming.

CHAPTER 19

CLAY: So you and Lois went to Mark Volpe's cabin after lights out.
AMBER: Yes.
CLAY: Did Lois administer one of these treatments to Mark that night?
AMBER: Yes.
CLAY: Did you assist her in that treatment?
AMBER: Well, I guess so. I ... did what I was told.
CLAY: Tell the jury about that treatment.

On the way to Mark's cabin, Lois attempted to enlighten Amber about Mark's medical problem. "Mark has a prostate problem," she explained. "There's a possibility that it can develop into cancer, but according to the doctor there's something he can do to greatly reduce his chances of it becoming cancer. We just need to do what we can to prevent that from happening."

"I see."

"Now I'm not exactly sure what he'll need you to do, but he assures me that you'll not have a problem helping him." There was a lengthy pause, and then she added, "I just can't seem to accomplish the same results as I used to."

"So you don't know what I'll need to do?"

"I don't know, exactly. But he'll tell you. It won't be difficult, I'm sure."

When they reached the cabin, Lois just opened the door and walked in. There was enough light in the room for Amber to see that Mark was lying on his bed, wearing just boxer shorts.

CLAY: And did you see what Lois was doing?

AMBER: I don't know. I stopped looking. I didn't open my eyes.

CLAY: What was Mark doing?

AMBER: He was massaging my breasts.

CLAY: Through your clothing?

AMBER: Yes. But he put his fingers between the buttons of my blouse.

CLAY: Was that all he did?

AMBER: No.

CLAY: What else did he do?

AMBER: He ... put his hand under my skirt and ... touched me there.

CLAY: How do you mean, *touched?*

AMBER: He pulled my panties down and ... massaged ..."

There was a stirring in the courtroom – a number of Way friends were leaving, and Marty Spinner was taking in the whole scene. There was nothing he loved more than observing tense situations where deep dark secrets were uncovered, like a suspenseful *who done what* detective movie. Edith and B.J. were watching Amber, transfixed. Hattie had her head bowed and her hands clasped in her lap. And the prosecutor stared, his mouth wide open.

CLAY: Did you go back a second time, to Mark's cabin?

AMBER: No. The next time Lois asked I told her I was really sick.

CLAY: Were you sick?

AMBER: Yes. I almost vomited when she asked me to go again.

CLAY: So what happened when you didn't go back again?

AMBER: I complained that I had problems breathing and pains, and I got to go to a doctor the following day. I forget what I told the doctor, but he told me I had to go somewhere and rest, away from retreat. So I went to live with my brother, B.J.

CLAY: Why did you decide to return to the ministry?

AMBER: I thought I didn't have any options. I heard that Mark didn't have his own cabin at the new retreat place in Poppy Hill, so I thought it would be safe for me to go back. And Uncle Floyd let me go back. I didn't tell him about Mark.

CLAY: Why would you not tell Floyd about Mark, or Lois?

AMBER: I'd never tell him anything negative about anyone.

CLAY: Never?

AMBER: Never.

CLAY: Why not?

AMBER: I had no idea what his response would be. I didn't know if he'd even believe it. I wasn't supposed to know anything that he didn't know. He didn't like to be corrected.

CLAY: So tell us why you took the handgun with you to the service.

AMBER: B.J. didn't approve of me going back into the service, and he actually forbade me to go back without the handgun. I'd told him exactly what happened to me, and he told me he didn't want to ever hear about it happening again. He made me promise to use it if anyone tried anything again.

CLAY: How did you feel about that?

AMBER: I didn't like the idea, but I really didn't expect to have to use it. So I figured no one would ever know I had it.

CLAY: Tell the jury about the night Orville Voigt was shot.

AMBER: I was just going to the restroom and I saw a man in the dark coming into the yard between the dorm and the restroom. There was no reason for a man to be there. I just took out my gun and shot. I didn't even aim, I don't think. I thought it maybe wouldn't fire, but it did.

CLAY: Did you know who it was?

AMBER: No. It was too dark.

PROSECUTOR: Why were you so afraid to tell your superior about this incident in the cabin?

AMBER: All the handmaidens are afraid. We *never* spoke about anything negative.

PROSECUTOR: But Mark Volpe wasn't your head servant at that time.

AMBER: We thought he was. Uncle Floyd had still not died, but Mark was a man, and he would know what I said about him to Uncle Floyd, and ... I felt I was trapped into saying nothing.

PROSECUTOR: This fear, was it only about sexual matters or was it about other matters as well?

AMBER: It was about everything.

PROSECUTOR: Everything?

AMBER: Yes.

PROSECUTOR: For example ...

AMBER: One time two other handmaidens and I were in the back seat of a car and Uncle Floyd was driving, and a servant was in the front seat beside him. Uncle Floyd stopped for gas, and I knew he was supposed to be putting diesel fuel into that car, but he put regular gas in it instead. And the other handmaidens wouldn't let me tell him the difference.

PROSECUTOR: So you let him put the wrong fuel in the car! (He yelled.)

AMBER: (After a long pause, she yelled angrily.) I told you we were afraid of everything. You asked for an example, and I gave you one. I have a book full of examples why I was afraid. It's somewhere here in the court ...

The judge was startled. The courtroom was perfectly silent. Amber hadn't raised her voice throughout all of her testimony.

The prosecutor also looked startled. He said, "I have no more questions, Your Honor."

At the signal that her time on the stand had finished, Amber burst into tears, and sobbed loudly while Clay accompanied her to their table.

That evening an assembly of Way friends met in their bishop's home in Oildale, just north of Bakersfield. Most of those in attendance were working class couples with children, and had no opportunity to attend trials. For sure many of them had heard tidbits of what was going on in the courtroom that week, but one would never know from the content of the service.

There was the usual singing of hymns, the prayers, and then the humble testimonies of all who had confessed. For the most part, testimonies consisted of a short passage of scripture followed by the inspiring thoughts the reader had concerning the passage.

A couple of teenagers had found passages encouraging them to withstand the evil influences they encountered among their schoolmates. Another teenager had received a new insight into the necessity of prayer, and made known her desire to be more faithful in prayer.

One of the men had a very unpleasant experience at work – he didn't say what it was – and he lamented that he hadn't handled the situation in a more Christlike manner. His wife related that she'd witnessed the moral failures of a neighborhood woman and the consequences to her marriage, and she reviewed scripture that assured her of the superiority of Way friends' practices.

An elderly lady spoke of the time when her parents first encountered two Way servants, and the freedom and joy she and her family had because they had followed the servants. It was a testimony of such sincere gratitude, one the others in the assembly had heard many times before.

A couple of people mentioned the upcoming days of retreat in Poppy Hill, and the great need and expectation they felt for the benefits of those days. There were also a number of prayers for the success of the retreat, and the thankfulness they felt for the sacrifice of the servants and handmaidens who gave up everything to be able to lead them in following Jesus' example. The bishop gave special thanks for servants from other states and countries to bring their special messages to the Way friends in southern California. Several prayed that others in the world would come to appreciate the sacrifice of Jesus, and come to the Way.

The spirit of the gathering was one of humbleness, and it was obvious that everyone was pleased to be in the company of the others. When the service was over, however, things were not so quiet. They didn't become boisterous – they just became more animated.

Because it was still light outside, the smaller kids went out in the yard and played *Alley-Over*. Some of the mothers were afraid a stray ball would some evening break a window in the house, but fortunately that never happened. The teenagers congregated in one area of the room and conducted their teen-talk session, and made plans for the next time they could get together for some recreation.

Among the adults there was serious discussion about the trial. Everyone was quite upset that such a thing had occurred, and lamented the embarrassment they felt because it was such a bad mark on the reputation of the Way. There was no real discussion of anyone's guilt or innocense – the greatest concern was to protect children from any knowledge of the trial, and to avoid having their neighbors and acquaintances connect them to the court proceedings. That was made difficult by the mention of the shooting and trial in the news media. But they were depending on their own reputations to prevent themselves from becoming implicated in the immorality that was being aired. None of them, however, believed the Way would get a fair evaluation in the media.

When the court recessed for lunch that day, the prosecutor said to Clay, "I still think you're out of order with all of your witnesses."
"Hey," Clay replied. "The diary was *your* exhibit."
"I don't believe this." The prosecutor raised his hands in exasperation.
"Hang around," Clay advised. "I'll help you."

CHAPTER 20

In Poppy Hill the next day the servants gathered as usual in the dining hall for lunch. Tina had returned from Bakersfield – she'd stayed overnight with her cousin, claiming to be too exhausted to go back to Poppy Hill any earlier. Hattie, of course, still had not come back, but by then everyone had accepted that she wouldn't be coming back until Amber's trial was over. In any case, she wasn't strong enough to be of a great help with the site preparations.

Bart Stanley had returned. He'd muttered to a couple of servants that Mark had ordered him back to Poppy Hill, upsetting his attempts to *be of assistance* to whoever would talk to him in Bakersfield. Orville was there as well. He'd come back from Bishop in the expectation of being called back into court, but the call never came. He decided he'd stay at the retreat property in the expectation of having an assignment for the next season.

"Where's Lois?" someone asked.

"She had to go to Bakersfield this morning," Mark explained. He made no further comment.

As everyone was finishing up with their meal, Mark stood and called for everyone's attention. "I want to talk to you about a matter that's become a great concern to me," he began. "I've learned that the diary the police took from Amber's suitcase is where they found all the names of people to call for the trial. I don't know what all she could have written in it, but it's obvious the prosecutor used things she wrote to prove that she had a motive for shooting someone. That's why this thing got so out of control, and so many people ended up being implicated."

Orville and Tina were uncomfortable, even embarrassed.

"But Uncle Mark," an older servant interrupted. "Wasn't it Clay who called the others to testify?"

"Yes," Mark acknowledged.

"That's true," Bart interjected; but said nothing more.

Mark hesitated, then said, "I wish Clay had never become involved in this matter. But as I've said, Clay's involvement has made this an even more important matter. It would be good if none of us keeps such a diary, or records of things that occur among us. We see now that when the police have reason they can take any of our private thoughts and use them for any purposes they chose. So I'd like if any of you are keeping such notes or diaries or records, or whatever, that you dispose of them."

"I have a little photo album and I have 52 pictures in it," an elderly handmaiden worried. "My 52 companion handmaidens. Do I have to dispose of that?"

Mark didn't know what to say.

"It's only pictures," she assured him.

"It's what we write that can be the problem," Mark decided. "The best policy is to make sure we write nothing about anyone. We just have no idea when and how we can get in trouble when it gets read by someone else. What they've done with his trial is a good example of how our words can just come back to bite us, and can really do damage to the ministry when they're in the wrong hands."

Rocky nudged Gordon and whispered, "You keep a diary, little fella?"

"I can't even spell diary." Gordon replied.

"I always felt there was something not right about keeping a diary," Wilda confessed. "I guess I was being led aright."

Rocky looked at Gordon and pursed his lips as though to kiss. Fortunately no one else noticed his response to Wilda's fawning expression.

Gordon smiled and winked back!

There was little more conversation, and everyone took their dishes to be washed and dispersed to their chores.

"We're gonna need to check the trash cans tonight," Gordon said to Rocky. "Whose diary do *you* want to read?"

Clay called Lois Snyder to the stand. She came in, looking terrified, and playing with her hands nervously. After she was properly identified, Mark began asking her questions. It was obvious to everyone present that he was having a hard time getting the answers he wanted. Abruptly he turned to the judge and asked to have her declared a hostile witness.

"I did *not* commit a crime," Lois cried.

"No, ma'am," the judge responded. "That's not the point."

A conversation ensued, among the judge, the prosecutor, and Clay, that no one else in the courtroom understood. Then the judge announced, "Mr. Shipman, I will grant your request. You may proceed."

Clay began by asking Lois questions about the role of different members of the Way ministry, and how the ministry operated.

Lois explained that Mark Volpe was the head servant, and he directed all the affairs of the ministry in California. She said that Mark decided who'd be allowed to enter the ministry, what each person would be assigned to do, what area of the state each one would be assigned to work in, and for how long.

LOIS: Everyone does what Uncle Mark tells them to do.

CLAY: Is there ever discussion among all the servants about any problems that individuals have?

LOIS: No.

CLAY: Do all the servants and handmaidens discuss questions of doctrine and policy together?

LOIS: Well, not discuss. Uncle Mark has meetings to tell us things we need to know ... and do.

CLAY: What input do you personally have on such matters as doctrine and policy?

LOIS: None, really.

CLAY: Why not?

LOIS: It's not in God's order for women to speak in the church.

CLAY: What about the younger servants?

LOIS: No, because they're just novices.

CLAY: Let's say you have a problem that involves you personally. Who do you go to about that kind of problem?

LOIS: Uncle Mark.

CLAY: For all problems?

LOIS: Yes. Well, for trivial things I discuss that with other senior handmaidens.

CLAY: What about a health problem?

LOIS: If I have a health problem, I speak to the head servant and he'll tell me what treatment I can have.

CLAY: Does he recommend a doctor for you?

LOIS: Yes. Uncle Floyd has recommended doctors for me.

CLAY: Has a head servant ever refused treatment for you?

LOIS: No.

CLAY: Have you ever been to see a doctor named Lucas Berta, in San José?

LOIS: (She looked shocked.) Yes.

CLAY: Did Uncle Floyd recommend that doctor ... by name?

LOIS: Not by name.

CLAY: Did he recommend any other doctor for treatment at that time?

LOIS: Uncle Floyd told me ... I told him I needed to see a psychological counselor ... and he told me I couldn't see one.

CLAY: So did you just go to Dr. Berta on your own?

LOIS: No. Well, I told Uncle Floyd that if I couldn't have some counseling that I'd not be able to continue in the service. That's when he said I could see a doctor that might be paid for by the government. I had no option. I couldn't afford anyone else.

CLAY: You had no income?

LOIS: I had what some of our friends would give me, but I was never supposed to keep more than two hundred dollars for myself.

CLAY: What if you were given more than two hundred dollars?

LOIS: I was supposed to send the rest to Uncle Floyd.

Clay's next line of questioning was about how she dealt with direction from the head servant, and from the older handmaidens who were her mission companions. Lois was very adamant that it was her duty to follow all directions.

CLAY: Whether you believe that direction is right or wrong?

LOIS: Well, yes. It's not given to women to have the same revelation as men.

CLAY: What if you decided to disobey a direction?

LOIS: If it was something important, well, I'd have to leave, of course. Things would never work if we all decided to do our own thing. Disobedient people are of no use to the Lord.

CLAY: In your experience in the Way ministry, whose direction would a servant or handmaiden be expected to follow?

LOIS: The head servant, the other servants after they'd been in the service for a while, and my more senior handmaidens.

CLAY: Is this true for all handmaidens, or is it just your experience in the ministry?

LOIS: Oh no. It's the same for all handmaidens. We have to submit, to be models of submission.

CLAY: Now, this court has been told about a treatment that you've been administering to Mark Volpe. Is that true?

LOIS: Yes.

CLAY: Can you tell us about that?

LOIS: What do you want to know?

CLAY: Were you directed to administer this treatment?

LOIS: Uh … Uncle Mark asked me.

CLAY: Did he ask you, or did he direct you?

LOIS: Well, he asked. He never orders anyone to do anything.

CLAY: But no one refuses?

LOIS: It's a matter of being willing, submitting.

CLAY: And this is the case for all handmaidens?

LOIS: Yes. All the handmaidens, and servants as well.

Clay paused for a couple of minutes.

CLAY: Now, this court has been told that this treatment you were administering to Mark Volpe was a preventative measure against prostate cancer. Am I right?

LOIS: Yes. (She was becoming flustered and very red faced.)

CLAY: What did this treatment involve? I presume it wasn't just giving him a pill.

LOIS: (She almost choked.) I'd like not to talk about that.

CLAY: Your Honor, I require answers to these questions.

JUDGE: Please answer the question, Miss Snyder.

CLAY: What did this treatment involve?

LOIS: He needed to relieve some pressure.

CLAY: Pressure where?

LOIS: (She lowered her head.) His prostate.

CLAY: Did this involve contact with his genitals?

LOIS: Yes.

CLAY: Did this treatment involve any medical devices?

LOIS: No.

CLAY: Were either you or Mark Volpe advised by Floyd Toner to deliver or receive this treatment?

LOIS: No.

CLAY: Were you having a romantic affair with Mr. Volpe?

LOIS: No.

CLAY: This was nothing more than a prostate treatment. Am I right?

LOIS: Yes.

CLAY: Did you not suspect that this was just a ploy to have you satisfy his sexual desires?

LOIS: No ... I don't know.

CLAY: Did it occur to you to refuse to administer this treatment?

LOIS: At first, maybe. No. I couldn't say no.

CLAY: Why not?

LOIS: I couldn't think of a good reason to say no.

CLAY: It occurs to me that Mr. Volpe could have provided this treatment for himself.

Lois made no comment.

CLAY: Is this kind of sexual contact acceptable according to the Way's moral code?

LOIS: Uh, not normally, I'm quite sure.

CLAY: If I may ask, how did you reconcile this request with your sense of morality?

LOIS: I had to make myself think of it as a kind of nursing task, I guess. Once I thought he should ask one of the servants to do it for him, but ... I don't know.

CLAY: Do you know why Mr. Volpe didn't take care of this problem by himself, if you know what I mean?

LOIS: I think he didn't believe in doing that.

CLAY: So he asked you to do it for him.

LOIS: Yes.

There was a pause.

CLAY: Who asked Miss Kite to assist in this treatment?
LOIS: I did.
CLAY: Why did you ask her?
LOIS: Mark told me to ask her. She was noted for her faithfulness and obedience.
CLAY: So why was Miss Kite's presence necessary?
LOIS: Well, uh, I ... She's young. Mark said he needed ... you know ... something to make it work.
CLAY: What about it wasn't working?
LOIS: Oh. I'm not young any more. (She put her hand over her mouth and continued.) He needed someone to ... I can't say that. (She paused.) Amber was very pretty.
CLAY: So shall we conclude that, as you understand this treatment, the real purpose for inviting Miss Kite to this treatment was to enable Mr. Volpe to have an erection?
LOIS: Yes. (She slapped her hand over her mouth again.)

The prosecutor tapped his pen on his note pad, and huddled with his fellow counsel. There was some shaking of heads, and then the prosecutor announced, "We have no questions for Miss Snyder, Your Honor."

And Lois was allowed to leave.

Lois was thoroughly embarrassed – she left the room without making eye contact with anyone.

And the judge called for a brief recess.

Clay left the courtroom and found Lois sitting alone on a sofa in the large waiting room. She looked distraught, and lowered her eyes when she saw him. He crossed the room and sat down beside her. "Lois," he said quietly. "I'm sorry I had to put you through this."

There were tears in her eyes, and she lowered her gaze again to her hands.

"You have no idea how sorry I am about the position you've been placed in. I believe every word you said in that room. This will change the rest of your life, won't it?"

Lois nodded her head.

I have never seen a more defeated woman in my life, Clay thought. "Do you have someone with you today? Someone who's coming for you?"

"The Hammonds are somewhere in the building. I'm supposed to meet them here."

"Lois, I have no idea what your thoughts are right now, but you're going to need some help, and I want you to come to me for anything you need. And I mean *anything*. I don't want to hear that you've been subjected to such abuse by Mark Volpe again, and I don't want to hear you've been denied any care you need."

Lois nodded, and wiped tears from her eyes.

"Mark needs to be stopped. I want you to consider making a formal complaint about him to law enforcement. I'll help you. I want to do something to help you. You have a standing invitation to my home. Keep this." He handed her a business card. "Promise me you'll use this."

Lois gasped deeply, and nodded her head.

"Here come the Hammonds," Clay said. "Hi, folks."

They shook hands timidly.

"Lois needs some TLC," Clay said. "You can do that, I'm sure."

"We certainly will," Mrs. Hammond said.

CHAPTER 21

Mark Volpe decided, on the advice of Percy Law, that something needed to be done to squelch all discussion about the trial in Bakersfield. They agreed that if nothing was done to counter the rumormongers, they could inflict any amount of damage to the reputation of the ministry.

They decided to call together all five assemblies in the Bakersfield area for a collective Sunday fellowship gathering, and both Mark and Percy would be there to speak to the Way friends. That way they'd be able to speak to everyone in the area before retreat, and hopefully succeed in having people concentrate more on the upcoming retreat than on the trial.

Before Victor Bergman had moved to Poppy Hill he'd lived in Bakersfield, and he still owned some properties there. When asked about possible venues for the Sunday occasion, he volunteered to help, and within an hour he'd reserved the club house in the gated community of his Bakersfield residence. It had kitchen facilities and was permitted to accommodate 200 people at a time.

The five bishops around Bakersfield were then called and given the responsibility of informing their congregations about the special gathering.

In the courtroom, the prosecutor was delivering his closing arguments. It was quite straightforward, according to him. He held a pen in his hand, and gestured and pointed and loudly emphasized each point he was making.

He reminded the jury that Amber Kite had been *bellyaching* for years, in her diary. All but one of the people she'd complained about was someone in authority over her in the Way, and all but one was a man. And the person accused of assaulting her was Mark Volpe – did anyone on the jury believe that what Orville had done in *any* way resembled what Mark had done? He asked the jury to disbelieve Amber's claim that she'd been too afraid to run – she was *not* too frozen by fear to pull out a gun and shoot with it.

Furthermore, Amber had carried the gun secretly with her for over a year, and had also admitted she'd made a promise to use it. And she also admitted that Orville had made no threatening gesture, other than to begin walking in her direction. In closing, he assured the jury that he'd successfully proven every element of the crime of attempted murder. And concerning the charge of illegal possession of a handgun, Amber had frankly admitted to that.

Clay whispered something to Amber, and she smiled slightly. When he rose to speak, he calmly approached the jury, and in a quit manner began to address them. He immediately captured their undivided attention ... he spoke low enough that a couple of them had to lean forward to hear.

"Ladies and gentlemen, you are charged with determining whether Amber Kite intended to murder Orville Voigt ... or not! But before you come to that decision, you need to consider how you would expect your own twenty five year old daughter to react, alone outside in the middle of the night, in the dark, when some very large unidentified man approaches her to within twenty feet." There were seven middle aged men and women on the jury, all of them wearing wedding rings; and who probably had a daughter, or son, of their own over whom they'd anguished late at night. "Twenty feet, and approaching. Does she have time to ask him who he is? Or should she try to get back to her dorm door, which would mean running past the man to get there? Or should she turn her back to him and trust that she surely can outrun him? Or what?

"From all the testimony you've heard, you have *not* heard that Miss Kite would expect any man on the property that night to go into the women's restroom. Moreover, Mr. Voigt assured us that he certainly did know where the men's room was, and that it was *closer* to his dorm than it was to the women's dorm. But it doesn't matter what reason Mr. Voigt had for being in the women's restroom, Miss Kite did not know who he was, say nothing about why he was there. No one but a stranger could be expected to arrive in that manner at that restroom that night."

Clay never looked anywhere but in the faces of the jurors. He didn't even lower his gaze while he stepped sideways to relax his stance. He wouldn't let them look away … anyone who looked away he'd give uninterrupted eye contact until he was sure the juror was going to pay attention. It was Clay's closing paragraph that would rankle the Way servants and friends most, and get widely published in the Way friends' rumor mill, even if the servants asked for silence on the matter.

"Big cities have crime problems. But there's a crime problem in Poppy Hill. During this trial we have examined events in only five four-day retreats, in sequence, a total of twenty days. During that time there were three property crimes – unreported though they were. Last year Los Angeles reported 137,099 property crimes, in a population of four million in a period of 365 days. Compared with the crime rate in Los Angeles, the three property crimes in twenty days translates into 216,000 per year compared to L.A.'s 137,000 per year. It may be safer to park your car in L.A. overnight.

"At the same five sequential Way retreats we also encountered a minimum of six instances of crimes of violence – crimes against individuals. That rate of assaults against individuals translates into 432,000 a year compared to 51,242 reported in Los Angeles in a year. Should I suggest that anyone who thinks it's safe for a young woman to go out by herself at midnight in Poppy Hill should better take her midnight stroll in L.A. instead?

"We've had enough testimony in this trial to convince anyone that Miss Kite is anything but a violent person. She was not out at night looking for *anyone* to kill. She went out to use the restroom, and without warning found she had to defend herself, and she had nothing else to defend herself with."

When he finished, there was a dead silence in the courtroom – he had so quietly addressed the jury that no one dared shuffle his feet in case he'd miss something.

"Do you think you convinced the jury?" Marty asked?

"Oh yes," Clay replied. "One way or another," he smiled.

"What if you lose?"

Clay looked right into Marty's face. "Lose what?"

"This case."

"We've already won more than we could lose."

"I don't get it."

"Can you imagine the shit that will fly in Poppy Hill tonight? This is just the first little gremlin to pop out of Pandora's diary. In the end Amber's going to be better off than a lot of others."

"Yeah?"

"Oh, yeah. I hope I don't have to do this, but you know what I'd really like to get my teeth into? If Amber's found guilty, I'll get to address the judge concerning her punishment." He paused. "I can use an opportunity like that."

"What for?"

"Some people never get to speak for themselves. I have something I've been wanting to say."

"How long do you think they'll deliberate?"

"Who knows? I need a sleep."

"Are you going somewhere?"

"No. I'm going to find a comfortable chair and go to sleep."

"You can go to sleep now? I'm so hyped up I doubt if I'll even sleep tonight."

"I go to sleep when I want," Clay smiled. "It relaxes me."

Most people in California had never heard of a place called Poppy Hill. Anyway, who cared about a hamlet of maybe 200 people away out in the desert? Strange and dreadful things happen to people who venture that far from civilization, and Californians were used to the notion that society's dissenters and weirdos liked the desert. The Kite trial was such another tale from the desert.

What created public interest in the trial wasn't the fact that it was an attempted murder trial, it was because there was some sort of kinky ritual being performed. The news that evening would surely bolster the desert's reputation for harboring the eccentric and mysterious.

The announcer began, "In Superior Court this afternoon, the case of the Kite attempted murder trial was given to the jury, who are at this time deliberating on the fate of Miss Amber Kite. Miss Kite is the young woman who was a cleric of some rank in a religious community based in Poppy Hill, a very small community in the Mojave Desert. Miss Kite is accused of shooting with the intent to murder another young cleric by the name of Orville Voigt a year ago at their desert compound. Miss Kite and Mr. Voigt were fellow clerics, and by coincidence cousins.

"The defense today succeeded in hearing evidence about unusual sexual practices that were carried out at the Poppy Hill location. We'll go now to Jock Miller, who is in Poppy Hill at the entrance to the sect's compound there. Jock, what can you tell us about what is happening there now?"

"Hi." Jock appeared on the screen. "It's been really difficult knowing what's happening here. You'll see behind me that there's a mansion of a home sitting atop the hill, the hill that this community was named for, in fact. I went up there earlier in the day to see who I might engage in some conversation, but I was promptly asked to leave the property. The property line is right here where this private drive opens onto this state road."

"Has there been any traffic onto or off the property at all?"

"A few cars have come and a few others have left, but no one was interested in saying anything to me. I did get to speak to a couple of curious neighbors, though. One young lady stopped to talk for a minute. She had some rather complimentary things to say about these people."

"They're nice people," the young lady explained. "We never see them except a couple of times a year, and they never bother anyone. They're a little old fashioned, but I'd never have thought they did any of those strange things up there."

Jock returned to the screen. "On the other hand," he smiled, "an older gentleman came by a few minutes ago. He didn't want to be named, but he did want to have his say."

A disheveled middle aged man began speaking. "I think they's all crazy up thar. I went up thar one time and thar was these two fellas by the pond, up thar. And they just took all they's clothes off and got butt nekkid and went swimmin'. I thought they was gonna get queer, but they didn't. I don't know whar those people come from."

"So you see, we have mixed thoughts among the residents out here. I've been informed that by Wednesday of next week the traffic here will increase greatly with people coming from all over southern California for the semi-annual retreat."

"Thank you, Jock, for keeping us updated."

Trent Hanson immediately grabbed his phone and called Aaron Finkelstein. "Did you see Buzz Crowe on the news?"

"No."

"He's the one who saw us skinny dipping that day in Poppy Hill."

"Oh, no?"

"Yeah, he was on the news. He told the reporter that he thought we were going to *get queer*, but we didn't."

Trent and Aaron had a great laugh. They'd been novice servants at the time, assisting with the construction of the retreat facilities, and had taken advantage of the pond to have a swim to cool off on a blistering summer afternoon. They'd never told anyone about their swim, but they always wondered how the rumor about the event ever got started.

"I'm gonna call Marty Spinner," Trent said.

Marty's response was, "Hey, I have an idea. You wanna have some fun next week?"

CHAPTER 22

Saturday at noon, as all the servants were finishing their lunch, Mark Volpe's cell phone rang. He answered, but his side of the conversation amounted to only a few words. The expression on his face told everyone it was anything but a friendly little chat. Then he thanked the caller and put his phone away. "There's a verdict," he said.

Everyone stopped moving. No one said a word.

"Not guilty," he announced.

There was an extended period of silence, then people all wanted to speak at once.

"I'm so glad!"

"Good! This is over!"

Most of the comments were of relief, but Bart wasn't so sure. "Now someone else will think they can bring a gun to retreat."

"How do you feel, Orville?"

"I think I feel harassed." He looked embarrassed.

And people got quiet again, anticipating Mark's directive on how to assess the situation.

Lois was wiping her eyes, and Tina got up and left.

But Mark slipped quietly out of sight.

A reporter caught one of the jurors as she was leaving the courthouse. She was a middle aged woman, plainly dressed, and Clay's idea of a concerned mother.

"Excuse me, ma'am," the reported called. "Do you mind if I ask you a few questions?"

"I guess so," the juror replied. "I can always refuse to answer, can't I?"

"Sure. Tell me how you feel about being on this jury?"

There was a long pause. "I feel good."

"It took you eight hours to reach a verdict. You must not have had a difficult time coming to your decision."

"*I* seriously had no problem deciding."

"But some others did?"

"Damn right. A couple of them wanted her executed immediately. But by the time the rest of us set them straight about all the goddam predators crawling around at night, we had no problem finding her not guilty. I think the other women out there need guns too. And that slimy old bastard that runs the place .... I have to go." And she turned and walked away.

The clip appeared on the news that evening.

Sunday morning all the Way friends in the Bakersfield area assemblies gathered in the club house for fellowship as arranged. Everything was the same as any other Sunday, just a lot more people. The kids were excited because they got to see all the Way kids in the area, which didn't happen all that often. The women were having a great time setting up for the meal. Since it was a big gathering, many of them had tried to outdo themselves by bringing something more exotic or more delicious than they'd ever brought before.

The men were visiting as well, while they were arranging tables and seating. No one mentioned the trial. It was undoubtedly because they expected that Mark Volpe would be walking in at any minute and they didn't want to get caught discussing the matter.

The teenagers were huddled on the tennis court. When they first arrived there were some attempts at getting a tennis match going, but it wasn't long before a couple of them were huddling, and the rest of them had to go and see what was happening.

One kid, Keith, claimed to know everything there was to know about the trial. He wouldn't tell anyone where he'd found out, but claimed to have overheard someone telling someone else what really went on in Poppy Hill. "You'll not believe this," he told them, and proceeded to lay out his version of everything that happened. The others were all horrified. And some of them thought it was the best gossip they'd heard in a long, long time.

The girls mostly voiced utter disgust, and a couple of them decided Keith was lying and made sure everyone heard them say it. A couple of the boys, however, didn't let the girls' prevent them from offering their usual racy remarks.

"Who ever thought the head servant would be so horny?"

"Do you suppose Uncle Floyd had a girlfriend too?"

"Just imagine, Lois Snyder. Yuck!"

"I always wondered what they did in those cabins in the orchard."

"If you guys don't stop, I'm going to tell my parents on you."

Two of the bishops got off by themselves and dared to mention the trial. "What do you think of this Poppy Hill thing?" Jim asked.

"Does everyone here know all about this?"

"I'll guess most of them know nothing. I'm glad Amber got off, but can you imagine your little girl growing up and going in the service and being confronted with that kind of sick stuff?"

"I just have this urge to go to that man and give him a real piece of my mind. I just want him to disappear before someone else dares to force him to disappear."

"I feel the same. I would, but I don't dare do it while I'm so angry. I've thought about waiting until after retreat and then going to him. I hope I'm in a better frame of mind by then."

"He's got to be stopped, and who's going to do it? It's probably going to be up to us. Who else is going to do anything about it? They know what the consequences of that would be."

Mark and Percy walked into the hall.

"We'll talk later."

"Yes."

It was Percy who addressed the gathering that day. "It's a pleasure for me to be here with you today. The food was wonderful, and I've enjoyed the fellowship immensely. But as you all will have suspected, Mark and I are here today to share just a few thoughts about the events of the past week.

"It's quite fortunate for us all that the trial ended the way it did. I'm sure God's hand was in the outcome. None of us wishes Amber anything but the best. Right now we all feel at a loss to know what we can do for her, but we can be sure that the Holy Spirit will deal with us in the future if there's some way for us to reach out to her.

"We're all aware, of course, that it's not Christlike to take our brother to the law, but sometimes it's not within our control whether our brother, or sister, will be arrested. I suppose the lesson here is that we have to be more aware of the fact that it's not just our brother who will report us to the law. People in the medical profession and people in the field of education have become more inclined to report people to the police, so we need to avoid that if we can.

"It was wise advice when Paul told us not to go to the law. What happens when the law gets involved is that far, far more is made of an incident than necessary, and it ends up hurting as many people as the law can reach. That's been a great problem for the servants during this trial, but it appears our friends in the Way were for the most part not implicated in this case. We servants have been very grateful for that.

"Now that the trial is over, and Amber has been acquitted of the charges against her, all of these things can be put behind us, and forgotten, so everyone can continue in the places God gave them. We'll remember, of course, that we need to mind our conversation, so that no one will dwell further on this case ... or give anyone outside the fold cause to speak against us.

"We need to hide ourselves in Christ so that it will be Christ that we will show to the world. I once was speaking to a man who was in a war, and he found himself in a situation where the enemy was about to surround him and there was nowhere for him to escape to. Then he saw a big abandoned barrel, and he climbed into it and stayed there until all danger was past. He compared it to hiding in Christ. As long as he stayed inside the barrel, all anyone could see was the barrel. So as long as we all abide in Christ, others will know nothing else about us but Christ.

"And of course your retreat is coming up this week. I'm sure you're all anxious to be there for all the help we're going to receive. It's also a real privilege to be here among you, and I certainly will have good things to tell people back in Colorado when I go home."

No one responded. No one asked questions. People gave approving smiles to each other, and some nods of agreement were shared. Jim and Corey glanced at each other and rolled their eyes.

In the few days before retreat opening, it remained for the most part as quiet as it always was in Poppy Hill. Some of the locals claimed they saw *city people* cruising through the community and looking all around. They suspected they were people curious to see where the strange cult was hanging out. It could have been true, because five or six unidentified cars drove up the hill to the retreat grounds, for no apparent reason, then quickly turned around in the yard and left.

As was the custom, on Wednesday a *RETREAT* sign was set up beside the road at the foot of the hill. There were always a few people coming to retreat who'd never been there before. In any case, it shouldn't have been a problem finding the place if one knew to look for the mansion atop the hill.

This time, however, another sign appeared at the foot of the hill. A battered old van arrived with a large sign pasted on the back of it – roof to bumper. The van was parked on the side of the main road with the sign facing toward Bakersfield, the route most people would use to come to retreat. The driver and passenger got out, checked to make sure the doors were locked, and walked a few hundred feet to *Dirty Gertie's*, Poppy Hill's only convenience store, gas station, and bar.

As was the custom, shortly after noon two young servants took up their position at the top of the hill to greet the retreat attendees as they arrived, and accept donations. And the cars began arriving.

It wasn't until the third car arrived that the two young servants were made aware of the unusual sign displayed at the foot of the hill. "You mean the *RETREAT* sign?" one of them asked the driver.

"Oh no," the driver said. "There's another sign. I can't repeat what it says for you."

So the two young servants went down the hill to check it out. To their horror, it read, *Uncle Mark screws around with handmaidens*.

CHAPTER 23

By seven o'clock that Wednesday evening a thousand people had congregated in the huge shed that had been built to accommodate the retreat. The crowd had become quiet, and many were perusing the program of speakers scheduled for the next four days. It wouldn't be long until the strains of four part harmony would again waft over the small community of Poppy Hill. It would be an indication to the citizens of the town that their twice annual visitors' four days of singing had begun. It had become a looked-forward to event in the otherwise quiet, sleepy community.

Dirty Gertie, whoever she was, had stocked up well on bottled water. The Way friends would be dropping in and buying it by the six-pack – their defense against the dry desert air. The manager had prepared for greater than usual gas sales that weekend, and a good supply of candy had been brought in. Twice daily a few dozen of the children would wander down to the store to buy a bag of candy. The children were usually very polite, and very welcome – you could ask them anything you wanted and they'd tell you what they knew.

Right on schedule at seven o'clock on Wednesday evening the service started. And as the cool desert evening air crept into the shed the familiar ambiance of the occasion settled in, and the fast paced busy world they'd all come from was for the moment replaced with this quiet, peaceful, restful event. The small children opened their doodling pads, and the teenagers adjusted for a comfortable posture, and looked around to see if all their good friends were there. Most people had brought blankets or cushions to pad the wooden benches they would be occupying for the four days.

As usual, at the end of that first service, Mark Volpe stepped onto the platform to make his usual retreat announcements. His first announcement was the usual one, the one that usually got ignored. "We'd like to ask everyone not to leave the retreat property between services this time. We're concerned that the children are in danger of being hurt in the traffic on the road down below, and we believe the influence of the community down there may not be best for them right now."

But he continued with a new admonition. "Also, we have concern that everyone respect the property of others. In the past some people have made known concerns about this, and we want to ensure that everyone's property is safe while we are together."

When he finished, everyone rose, and people began mingling and making their way to the dining area where they would enjoy a bedtime snack. Mark was standing in front of the platform, talking with Percy Law and Herman Green. Herman was the head servant in Arizona, and was there as a guest speaker for the retreat.

Marty Spinner walked up to Mark and interrupted. "Uncle Mark. I saw someone tearing a sign off a car on the road."

"On what road?"

"Right at the foot of the hill. Isn't that destruction of property?"

"What about it?" Mark was obviously annoyed.

"It was Ned Gore. And I think it was Lloyd Blair with him."

"They were greeting people at the top of the hill," Mark protested.

"Not when I saw them," Marty said. "They were tearing some big sign off someone's van, parked on the side of the road by *Dirty Gertie's*. You might want to talk to them about that." He moved on.

The rest of the retreat went normally. Well, a few unusual things happened. On Friday Mark Volpe's name was on the program, but Bart Stanley spoke to the crowd instead. Bart explained that Mark was *indisposed*. Lois Snyder had some kind of collapse during the afternoon service, and had to be taken out on a stretcher. Neither Tina nor Orville spoke to the congregation as scheduled, but since they were only allotted five minutes each, the main speaker for those services just spoke that much longer. Lois had not recovered soon enough to speak in the Saturday evening service, as scheduled.

On Saturday evening, when the new assignment list for the servants and handmaidens would normally have been posted on the bulletin board outside the retreat kitchen, there appeared a sign that read: *The assignment lists for the coming season will be mailed to your respective bishops.* Nonetheless, on Sunday evening all the Way friends returned to their homes throughout southern California – the stress of the past season apparently had been removed, and everyone was anticipating a good season ahead.

On Monday afternoon Victor Bergman met Eddie Draper, the head servant from Washington, and Farrell Wiener, the head servant from Oregon, at LAX and took them to Poppy Hill. No one was told about either their arrival or departure.

And lest we forget, when Edith arrived back at the Roxton home in La Cañada, Mrs. Roxton was overjoyed to have her back. "The children have missed you so much," she told Edith. "And I can hardly imagine how relieved you are with the verdict. We heard from a good friend in Bakersfield that the trial was over. I thought of you every moment you were gone."

"Thank you," Edith replied. "I'm so relieved."

Mrs. Roxton smiled. "And when you were gone a very handsome Dr. Kumar Tesfai came by, asking for you. He told me you'd know who he is, and he left his card for you. He put a number on the back of the card, and he wants you to call him."

Edith took the card, and stared at it for a long time. "Oh my!" she whispered, and brushed her hand over her eyes.

EPILOGUE

As expected, when Thursday came around all the bishops had the new list of servant assignments. It was a highly anticipated event – not unlike the first day of school when students clamor to find their place in the newly shuffled staff of teachers. The concerns were: What servant, or handmaiden, has been assigned to my city this time? What servant has been assigned to my good friend in some other city? Secretly, many people entertained thoughts like: Poor cousin Johnny, he's going to have to deal with Bart Stanley this season. Or: Lucky Daniel, he gets to have one of the coolest servants where he lives.

But there was other important information on the assignment list as well. It also reported who was new on the list, and who had been sent to another state. It also named the servants who had no assignments for the season, and the reason why not; for example: resting, caring for mother, etc. Sometimes the list would indicate such things as temporarily assigned to Montana. And this time the new list had its share of surprises.

At first glance, there appeared to be no changes in assignments at all. Everyone was returning to their previous assignment – with a few exceptions. Norman Coombs had been moved to Oklahoma, and Orville Voigt had been sent to Colorado. Lois Snyder was listed as resting. It was no surprise that Amber Kite's name did not appear, and it was somewhat of a surprise that Tina Malek's name was removed as well. But it was indeed a shock that Hattie Burk's name did not appear either – anywhere on the list. The seven names missing were replaced by five names of servants imported from other states, and two novices to the ministry. The list was nothing short of fodder for endless speculation and rumor.

Most times when a servant's name was removed from the list, he or she had either passed away or voluntarily left the ministry. Then, occasionally someone would ask why that servant left the ministry, and the usual answer was because of a nerve problem. It was a usual occurrence that servants and handmaidens were sent to other states, and few people ever asked why. Once in a while, though, someone would speculate that the move was for disciplinary purposes. But none of those suspicions could ever be proven to be true. But what had happened to Hattie and Mark?

It was a long time before the puzzle of Mark's disappearance was explained. It was learned that Percy Law had heard nothing about Mark's involvement in the Amber Kite case; that is, until Mark recruited Percy to help him investigate the sign incident. In that process, Ned Gore had told them exactly what the sign said, and Percy became more concerned about what the sign said than about the prank itself. Mark, feeling trapped, had to admit that damning testimony about him at the trial was true.

Over the next 48 hours Percy did his own investigation. He spoke to a number of people in attendance at the retreat, and filled out the scanty details Mark had given him about the court testimony. Before the retreat was over, Percy had contacted some head servants in other states and asked them to come immediately to Poppy Hill to address the situation.

The showdown Percy orchestrated occurred on Monday afternoon. Mark was accused, tried, ousted from his position in California, and send immediately to Illinois. In Illinois he was to be placed under the supervision of the head servant there. The other head servants present agreed that Farrell, because he was from Oregon, would for the time being assume responsibility for both Oregon and California. A meeting of a greater number of head servants would convene some time in the fall, and a new head servant would be appointed for California.

It turned out to be a difficult decision for some of the more tenured servants in California to accept. They realized that, before they'd even learned that Mark was being dethroned, the decision about how his successor would be selected had already been made.

None of them would dare protest the decision, of course, but a couple of the presumptive heirs apparent were nothing short of glum on hearing the news.

Amber Kite didn't even show up for retreat, so there was no question whether she wanted to continue in the ministry. Tina stayed for the whole retreat, but had informed Mark on Friday that she could no longer continue in the ministry. Hattie, however, was as surprised as anyone else that her name was not on the new assignment list.

When the list was distributed among the servants and handmaidens on Tuesday morning, Hattie asked Mark if it was a mistake that she couldn't find her name on the list.

"Oh, yes," Mark replied. "I forgot to tell you. There won't be any assignment for you this year."

Hattie was stunned. "Will I be resting?"

"If you wish, sure," Mark said. "You can do what you like now, you're on your own. Do you have anyone in mind that may want you to stay with them?"

"I hadn't thought of that."

"I'm sure a lot of friends would love to have you in their home."

Then someone distracted Mark, so he patted Hattie's shoulder and moved on.

Orville Voigt went to Colorado. He met his new servant companion the day he arrived, and they were doing well with their work in a small town in the northeastern part of the state. That was, until he had an emotional collapse about Thanksgiving time and demanded to be allowed to go home to Bishop to be with his parents. Because his breakdown was common knowledge, many people in California continued to ask about him, and express their concern. The next spring, however, he decided to move to Las Vegas, where Oliver lived, to find work. The inquiries about his well-being tapered off – undoubtedly because it was unheard of that anyone needing a safer spiritual environment would go to Las Vegas, of all places.

Lois Snyder endured the company in Poppy Hill until all the servants were leaving for their assigned locations. She asked for a ride with four other handmaidens who were leaving for Santa Barbara. They were to drop her off in Los Angeles. She had all her luggage, but didn't tell them exactly where she was going until they were approaching Santa Clarita.

"I need to be left off at the Amtrak station in L.A.," she abruptly announced. She hadn't participated in any of the conversation since they'd left Poppy Hill, and none of the others had asked what her plans were.

"Where are you going?"

"I just need to go to the Amtrak station," she repeated.

"We can take you anywhere you want, Lois," one of them assured her.

"You can't go to the train station. No one's expecting you there," another protested.

"I'll be fine," Lois assured them.

"Lois, please let us take you to one of our friends."

"There are all kinds of dangerous people at the train station."

"We want you to be safe."

"I'll be safe," Lois insisted.

The others in the car couldn't convince Lois of anything, so they took her to the train station. They helped her into the station with her luggage, and then asked if they could wait with her – until she got to do what she intended to do.

"No," she said. "Please go. I'm not sure how long it will take. You'll be too late getting to Santa Barbara."

But the others didn't really leave. They found a place to watch from a distance to see what she would do. As soon as they were out of sight, Lois pulled her cell phone out and called someone. When she finished talking she waited and waited.

About a half hour later a couple with two children approached Lois. They chatted briefly, then the husband picked up the heaviest of her luggage and they left the station.

"That's Clay Shipman," one of the handmaidens said.

"And Nancy."

"She's going home with them."

"Does Uncle Mark know about this?"

"I doubt it. I doubt we'll see her again, for a long time."

"Poor Lois."

"Well, at least she's not going to end up dead in some back alley tonight."

When they returned to their car, it was already getting dark, so they called the home in Santa Barbara where they were expected and informed them that they'd be arriving there much later than planned.

Lois went home with the Shipmans that night, and very little was heard of her after that. From time to time Clay would run into one of the Way friends and he'd tell people that Lois was well, and comfortable in a small studio apartment in Manhattan Beach.

Bart Stanley looked for Amber at retreat and, of course, didn't find her. He then looked for Edith, and didn't find her either. It was unlike Edith to miss retreat, and he was concerned. So when he learned he was to return to Fresno for the next season, he left immediately. In Fresno one of the bishops kept a car for the servants assigned to that city, and Bart went there first to get it. And he drove directly to La Cañada.

He raced to ring the door bell at the Roxton residence, and was escorted to a gazebo in the back yard near the pool.

"Edith," he said when he saw her. "Why weren't you at retreat?"

Edith stared at him, "I ..., I ... ."

"Who is this?" Bart asked, turning to the man sitting facing her.

The man rose. "Bart," he said, and extended his hand. "Don't you remember me? I'm Kumar Tesfai."

Bart ignored the extended hand. "What are you doing here?"

"I heard about what was going on with Edith's family and I decided I'd come and give her a visit. I haven't seen her in years."

"How long are you staying?" Bart asked.

"I'm retired. I'm just visiting places to see where I'd like to live now," Kumar said.

"I know why you're here," Bart said. "And I have something to say to you. You should not be here. This woman is not free to enter into a marriage with anyone – her husband is still alive and ..."

"Bart," Kumar interrupted. "Excuse me. It's not necessary for us to have this conversation. Edith and I are plenty old enough and competent enough to decide for ourselves. Is there anything else you wanted to speak to us about? We weren't really expecting you today."

"Yes, now that I think of it, where is your wife?"

"I never married."

"I'm not sure I can believe that."

"Bart," Kumar protested. "We don't want to have this discussion with you. Maybe you should leave us alone now."

Bart showed his shock at being dismissed, then turned and strode back into the house. As he raced to the front door and left, Mrs. Roxton became concerned and went to check on Edith and Kumar. "Are you two okay?" she asked them.

"Yes," Edith smiled. "Kumar and I are planning to …"

"Make up for lost time," Kumar finished the sentence, and kissed Edith on the forehead.

www.ingramcontent.com/pod-product-compliance
Lightning Source LLC
LaVergne TN
LVHW091550060526
838200LV00036B/769